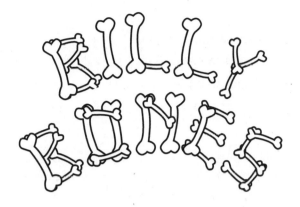

BILLY BONES

The Road to Nevermore

BILLY BONES

The Road to Nevermore

Christopher Lincoln

LITTLE, BROWN AND COMPANY
Books for Young Readers
New York   Boston

Little, Brown Books for Young Readers

Hachette Book Group
237 Park Avenue, New York, NY 10017
Visit our Web site at www.lb-kids.com

Little, Brown Books for Young Readers is a division of Hachette Book Group, Inc. The Little, Brown name and logo are trademarks of Hachette Book Group, Inc.

First Edition: August 2009

The characters and events portrayed in this book are fictitious. Any similarity to real persons, living or dead, is coincidental and not intended by the author.

Library of Congress Cataloging-in-Publication Data

Lincoln, Christopher, 1952–
    The road to Nevermore / by Christopher Lincoln.—1st ed.
        p. cm.—(Billy Bones)
    Summary: When Shadwick Gloom captures twelve-year-old Millicent and Uncle Grim and sends them to a hidden world within the Afterlife, it is up to ten-year-old Billy Bones to rescue them.
    ISBN 978-0-316-01475-5
    [1. Future life—Fiction. 2. Skeleton—Fiction. 3. Ghosts—Fiction. 4. Orphans—Fiction. 5. Supernatural—Fiction.] I. Title.
    PZ7.L654Roc 2009
    [Fic]—dc22

10 9 8 7 6 5 4 3 2 1

RRD-H

Printed in the United States of America

For Mary

Prologue
Celesdon Awaits You

By Gauzly Shimmer

The author's recent works include: WHEN TO BOW, WHEN TO BOO, *A Guide to Ghostly Manners,* **and HIGH SOCIETY ON HIGH**

If you can manage it, the best time to arrive in the Afterlife is late fall. That's when the city of Celesdon is most magnificent. The sun's low angle, sparkling through the jeweled domes and the water-rises of our capital city, is especially uplifting because, here in the next world, water flows up rather than falling down. It's a sight that can take your breath away, even if you have no breath in you.

As you disembark at the Hall of Reception, you will be granted a supply of golden wishes, the currency of the Afterlife. (If you're a skeleton, then unlucky you. Golden wishes are provided only to ghosts.)

You get only one "first time" in Celesdon, so make the most of it. My absolute favorite resting place is the Sapphire Plaza Hotel, located in the city's central ring. Service is heavenly.

Before checking in, I recommend shopping in the Glamoursmith district. That's where celebrated designers will fit you with shimmery fashions sure to suit the palest complexion. But be careful not to spend *too* many wishes. I speak from experience. I went through my allotment like a tyke in a toy shop! So take care, unless you want to spend an eternity earning a living by writing travelogues.

After you're properly outfitted, nothing is more memorable than flying up to the Sapphire in a royal carriage pulled by wind stallions.

As you alight, note the deep blue curved staircase — the one that seems to go on forever. You'll find golden wishes valuable here, too, because you can simply wish your way to the top. They're quite useful for getting around in general because the Afterlife is so impossibly big.

Once you're settled in, it's time to explore. I recommend the museums and even a visit to Government Hall. You need only crane your neck skyward to see this long structure. It spans the entire length of the Afterlife. One end houses Light Side officials, and the other end, the Dark. With that much building you might expect loads of government, and you wouldn't be wrong!

A word to the wise: all that governing produces a sea of regulation. And those who run afoul of the law are sent to a place much worse than the Dark Side.

Typically we only whisper its name (*it's called Nevermore*), and its location is shrouded in mystery. But no matter how murky the address, let me be clear: avoid it at all cost!

I won't gas on about *that* ghastly place, not with Light Side splendors to think of, like our floating boulevards, crystal courtyards, and cloud-packed parks. And I really shouldn't go on about those either, because they're for your later enjoyment. Much later.

So I shall leave you here with my greatest wish: Savor each day of a long, full life before you even think of a visit. These wonders will still be here long after you've done everything there is to do on Earth.

Part 1

Gloom Gathers

Upon a path, both straight and true
A bright heart, he has kept
It seems no matter where he treads
Gloom's shadow marks his step

Chapter 1
The Royal Dockyards at Barmouth

The ship creaked softly in a berth at Barmouth Harbor. Its bowsprit pointed out to sea like a finger, gauging wind and possibilities. Save for the shipwrights, the town was quiet. The proprietor of the cheese shop wiped his hands on his apron as he stood next to the fishmonger. For months they'd watched the birth of the ship. In two weeks, she would be fitted with canvas and brass. The shop owners smiled, proud that ship-making skills hadn't died in these parts. Steel and steam ruled shipyards now, but nothing pleased the eye like a wind-powered vessel.

A chunky ten-year-old clomped up the gangway. The sound of his boots blended with the snarl of saw blades and the cluck of mallets. A girl skipped behind him, shouting something lost to the wind.

Perhaps the shop owners would have looked less at

the ship and more at the boy if they'd known of his otherworldly past.

Billy leaned against the ship's bulwarks with a *thump*. "What's the use, Millicent? Everything a pirate could want is right here, but we're going to miss out."

Billy Bones Biglum and Millicent Hues were resting on the railings of the *Spurious II*. Billy's mother, Dame Biglum, was having it built to help promote her famous chocolates. The ship was soon heading out on a world-wide tour, and Dame Biglum had already engaged a real-life crew.

The children had begged to go along. They dearly wanted to see the world — every port, pack mule, and pyramid. But the old woman was adamant. "Lessons come first," she'd said. "Your education has been neglected far too long."

Millicent had never formally gone to school, although her parents had taught her the classics as well as music and art. During the twenty-five years Billy had lived in the secrets-closet, he hadn't aged a bit. He had, however, learned all sorts of things about the Afterlife, with the help of his skeleton parents. But Dame Biglum felt this kind of information wasn't terribly useful.

So she had hired a tutor.

Professor Digby Dabbleton was an older gentleman with a frosty beard and owlish eyes. He was an inventor whose workshop was jammed with curious things like submersible dinghies, rocket powered dirigibles, and life-size clockwork men. The children were quite fond of their instructor and his fascinating devices.

A shadow darted across the deck. Billy looked up to see a gull pass overhead, bound on its own secret journey. He sighed.

"A little patience," Millicent said. "I have a plan."

"You do?" Billy's brows lifted like curious caterpillars.

"Why don't we ask Mum Biglum if we can sail for just the summer?" Millicent beamed. "We'll be on holiday anyway."

The wind caught Billy's laugh and skipped it around the bay. "That's brilliant! There's nothing to do at home except get in her way. It's worth a shot."

"Oh Billy. It would be so grand!" Millicent swung herself up and sat on the rail. "Think how many places we'd explore."

"Where do you suppose we should go first?"

"Wherever the biggest mysteries are, of course. Egypt, maybe, or China." Millicent rubbed her forehead. This was her habit when cooking up plans. "But we'll promise her that we'll keep our noses buried in our summer reading. And you can't go blurting out the truth everywhere we go!"

It was the job of Billy's adoptive skeleton parents Lars and Decette Bones to collect and sort lies, secrets, and fibs. The Boneses were famous for their secret-keeping abilities. Billy, on the other hand, could rarely keep a tittle-tattle to himself.

"You know I'm working on that." Billy gave her a gentle nudge.

"Shush, Billy." Millicent dropped to the deck. "Here comes Mum Biglum."

Dame Biglum thumped over to join them at the rail. Her feet seemed bound on two different bearings, but with the aid of her silver-capped cane, she banged along with a determined stride. She wore a gray coat and a wide hat with pheasant feathers trawling off the back.

The old woman was both Billy's mother — in this life, anyway — and Millicent's grandmother. But to cut down on confusion, both children called her "Mum Biglum."

"Isn't she wonderful?" Mum Biglum proclaimed, tapping her cane on the ship's rail. "One of the shipwrights said he's never pinned a timber to a finer craft. The crew was most enthusiastic, too."

"I'd be more excited if *we* were going along," Billy sighed.

Millicent grabbed her grandmother's hands. "Could we could go, just for summer holiday? Maybe Professor Dabbleton could come along, too."

"We'd study every minute. . . . Professor Dabbleton would surely assign us loads of reading," Billy added. "Just think of all the time we could spend in lessons, and —"

"And out of my sight, and getting into trouble," Mum Biglum finished for him. "It's out of the question, my dears."

Both children slumped.

"Besides," she continued, "Professor Dabbleton wants to spend his holiday studying in Egypt."

"Egypt!" they cried in unison.

"*Alone*. The poor man needs some time to himself," said Mum Biglum with a thump of her cane. "As for today's business, our ever-prudent shipbuilder, Mr. Turnbuckle, told me the *Spurious II* will require several test runs before she's ready for open sea."

Billy plopped his forearm onto the railing and then his chin. Millicent frowned.

Mum Biglum's eyes twinkled. "Soooo . . . Mr. Turn-buckle has invited you on the first outing. You'll both have a two-day cruise."

Billy perked up. "Well, that *is* something!"

"Just the thing to get you two out of your soggy moods." Mum Biglum slipped an arm around each child.

Billy ran his hand over the hardwood railing. How he loved visiting the *Spurious II*! He remembered discovering the dusty plans for her predecessor, the *Spurious*. The ship's ancient blueprints had been tucked into a false bottom of the old sea chest he'd slept in so soundly the whole time he'd lived with his skeleton parents in the secrets-closet. It originally belonged to his great-many-greats grandfather Glass-Eyed Pete. The earlier *Spurious* was the first vessel he had pirated on, and even on parchment she looked formidable.

Now, several months later, Billy and Millicent were just weeks away from the *Spurious II*'s maiden sail.

Martha Cleansington chuffed up the gangplank like a steam-powered engine, carrying a loaded picnic basket. For years Martha had been one of the maids at High Manners Manor, but she was now the children's nanny. She had met Millicent only six months before, when the girl first arrived at the mansion — the poor orphaned granddaughter of Dame Biglum. Since then, Millicent had grown to a girl of twelve-and-three-quarters. Yet her pixie face and independent curls still carried the gentle brushstrokes of childhood.

Billy's history, on the other hand, was fuzzy to her. The boy had shown up, seemingly out of nowhere. It was odder than a bell without bongs because, according to the rumors circulating around the manor, he had gone missing twenty-five years earlier. And the boy hadn't aged a day. He still looked like a ten-year-old. Martha loved him dearly, so she didn't obsess on the strangeness. But still, it was most irregular.

Martha continued on at full power. "Pardon, madam, but Mr. Turnbuckle wishes to have a word about the extra accommodations he's working into the plans."

Dame Biglum nodded. "Well then, Martha, take care these two don't fall overboard."

"Don't worry, madam, I'll keep my eyes on 'em, tight as a glue pot's lid." Martha gathered her pewter-colored skirts and glanced at the upper deck. "They're like my own family."

"And so they are," Dame Biglum said, patting Martha on the shoulder. "Just as you're part of ours."

Dame Biglum set off for Mr. Turnbuckle's dockside office. Martha bravely grasped the railing and clambered up to the next deck. Her padded bustle swayed like it disagreed with every step. "Billy! Have a care!" she called out. "You'll split your melon if you take a tumble."

Billy was standing on an iron drum wrapped in anchor chain. "Oh Martha," Billy huffed. "How will I become the saltiest pirate on seven seas if I can't even have a good climb?" Then he danced a stout little jig until one foot skidded out from under him and he landed with a bum-rattling CLANG.

Martha pursed her lips. Billy abandoned the drum while Millicent stifled a laugh.

"Off we go, my ducks," Martha coaxed, gently turning Billy and Millicent toward shore. But the children insisted on "an explore," as they liked to say. All sorts of interesting discoveries beckoned from below deck, and the children were much too polite to refuse a good look. There, they found several new cabins — each just large enough to hold a bed, a sea trunk, and a small writing table.

"Goodness, children." Martha stationed her hands on her hips. "You could only sleep one eye at a time in a bed so tiny as that!"

The children didn't hear. They were poking their noses into every crack and corner. And, of course, they had to try out a bed. Billy and Millicent looked like cheery packed herring as they lay shoulder-to-shoulder and smiled.

"Let's be off for our lunch." Martha chuckled.

A few minutes later, the children were shoulder-to-shoulder again, this time, on a picnic blanket spread out on the town's pebbly beach. Billy and Millicent tore into sausage sandwiches and apple pie.

"It's nice to see such healthy appetites," Martha clucked. Then her eyes misted.

Billy and Millicent knew what was wrong at once. Just that morning Martha had learned her uncle was very sick. The children overheard her talking about it with Mr. Colter, the Biglums' new coachman. They nestled closer to Martha as they polished off the rest of their lunch.

Afterward, they strolled cobblestone streets until it was time to collect Dame Biglum.

"Mr. Turnbuckle needs to hire a captain," the old woman said, taking a hard look at the *Spurious II.* "He'll give me a list of candidates the next time we meet. I *do* hope we find someone who's steady. We don't want mutiny the first week."

As the children trailed the adults to the carriage, Billy whispered to Millicent, "What about Gramps Pete?"

"What about him?"

"He's a captain."

Millicent's eyes banged open. "Brilliant, Billy!"

"And if he's in charge, maybe he'd convince Mum Biglum to let *us* go."

"Even better!"

At the carriage, Billy struggled to hide his excitement as he stowed the picnic basket under the driver's bench. Mr. Colter helped Dame Biglum into her seat as the children gathered behind the carriage for a whispered conference.

"How are we going to get word to Gramps Pete?" Millicent asked. "He hasn't been around much lately."

Glass-Eyed Pete had been spending a lot more time in the Afterlife. This was no surprise, considering his long ordeal on Earth. The poor ghost had been trapped there the whole time Billy had been a skeleton. (A lengthy stretch for a spirit to be separated from the Afterlife.)

"But, you'd think he'd be back by now," Billy added, "and your parents, too."

"I know! I haven't seen them in weeks." Millicent frowned.

"What do you think is holding them up?"

"I'm not sure, but they're always complaining about the long lines."

"My mom and dad say there are plenty of those in the Afterlife," Billy agreed.

Millicent brightened. "Maybe your parents can help us post a note to Gramps Pete."

"Good idea. I'm sure Mr. Benders will deliver it." Billy smiled at the thought of the old skeleton messenger. He'd taught Billy many things about the Afterlife, whenever he popped by the secrets-closet.

"Let's sneak off to the secrets-closet tonight." Millicent smiled.

"What are you two plotting back there?"

The children spun round. Martha stood with hands on hips, but her frown was mostly smile. Martha wasn't gifted at seeing what ought *not* be there, like ghosts, so Billy, Millicent, and Dame Biglum never talked to her about such things.

"Nothing important," Millicent said quickly, before Billy could blurt the truth.

"Hmmm . . ." She scratched her nose. "Dame Biglum would like to head out." Martha shooed the children toward their seats. As she closed the shallow door the carriage lurched forward and clomped up the cobblestone streets, harnesses jingling like a banker's pockets.

A pleasant ride brought them back to High Manners Manor. It stood, waiting for them on the cliffs above the village of Houndstooth-on-Codswattle. The leaves on its ivy exterior rustled together as if they were tiny palms, impatient to see what new adventure was blowing their way.

Chapter 2
Sleep's Shadows

As the last toll of midnight was still reverberating, a dust speck floated along a dark hallway. It swirled past portraits of stately ancestors and through the keyhole of one particular bedroom door.

Inside this bedroom, the tall velvet curtains, hanging like calm sails, were drawn closed. Nearby, a large table was stacked with books: THE PIRATE WAY, by Black-Heart Bill; SHIVERING TIMBERS, by Evil-Eye Ned; and KNOW YOUR JIBE FROM YOUR JIB, by Bad-Penmanship Percy. Next to the reading material rested Billy's note. Like a buccaneer's dagger it was short and to the point:

Gramps Pete,
Come quick.
Billy

An unusual bed stood in the middle of the room, its headboard carved like a ship's stern. The foot of the bed rose to a point like the prow of a ship.

In the center of the mattress sat Billy's sea chest. He still preferred sleeping in his old trunk, even though it was a tight fit. Tonight, he tossed as if adrift in a storm.

"Noooooooo . . . ," he moaned. "Don't let him do that to you . . . Mom, Dad!" For the briefest moment, his eyes glowed blue and his bones lit up under his skin.

Billy sat upright.

A flutter of candlelight swung into his room. He scrambled out of his trunk, heart pounding like a shipwright's mallet.

"Shhhhhh, it's only me," Millicent hissed as she tiptoed toward the bed. "Quiet down, or Martha will hear."

Billy's hands shook. His wild hair pointed in every direction. "Sorry, Mill. It was another dream."

"You sure look a fright." Millicent swung the candle up to his face.

Billy winced. The light stung his eyes. "These dreams, they're more awful than you can imagine. Someone keeps taking Mom and Dad Bones away again . . . and hurting them."

"Billy, we've already seen the worst of the Afterlife. He's down in the sea trunk below." Millicent brushed her fingers through Billy's tangled hair.

Billy and Millicent had trapped Commissioner Pickerel, a particularly threatening Afterlife official, in the bowels of the manor. This was the biggest secret Billy had ever managed to keep. Only the children and Billy's ghostly gramps knew about it.

Billy rubbed his stomach. Since these dreams had started, it felt as if his insides were being cinched tight as a hangman's belt.

Millicent grabbed his hand. "Let's get down to the closet. You'll feel better once you see your parents." Millicent spun around. "I'll show you."

The floor creaked under their bare feet as Billy and Millicent passed through one of the many secret passageways riddling their ancient home.

Billy held tight to his note. He walked briskly to keep up and was nearly puffed out by the time they stood outside of the secrets-closet's sturdy door.

"Ready for family inspection?" Millicent grinned after fussing with the sash of her bathrobe.

"Very." Billy nodded and then told a truth, as was required to open the locked closet door. "I don't want to lose my parents again."

The key swung off its hook next to the door and twisted in the lock. The door groaned open. The closet was silent as a forgotten graveyard. For a panicked moment, Billy thought Mr. and Mrs. Bones *were* gone. "Mom? Dad?"

Mr. Bones's warm voice answered, "Look what a kind wind has blown our way, Decette. Visitors!"

Mrs. Bones clattered from the back of the closet. "Billy! Millicent! Do come in."

"Yes, straightaway," Mr. Bones abandoned his ever-present copy of the *Eternal Bugle*, his dependable source for Afterlife news, and held open his arms.

He wore a new silk vest, just the thing to carry the medal for distinguished service that he and Mrs. Bones had been awarded. Mrs. Bones was more modest about her medal. Hers was framed on top of her walnut filing cabinet.

Billy wrapped his skeleton father in a hug.

"Oooooofff . . . careful, my boy, you'll have me scattered in bits and pieces," Mr. Bones gasped. "Whatever is the matter?"

Millicent told him how she'd found Billy staggered by a nightmare.

Mr. Bones caressed Billy's cheek. "As you can see for yourself, here we stand. We won't be going anywhere soon."

Mrs. Bones descended on him with more hugs. "Oh, Pumpkin, don't worry."

Millicent mouthed "pumpkin" and giggled. Billy blushed.

"They won't even let us out for a long-promised vacation. The Department of Fibs and Fabrications has other concerns at the moment." Mr. Bones gave his wife a worried glance, then retrieved his pipe and turned toward the children.

"No more of this talk, eh? Seeing you two is our greatest pleasure. And hearing about all that's going on, well, it's like we've taken a stroll out of the closet ourselves." Mr. Bones rested a hand on Mrs. Bones's shawl. "Decette, why don't we have some cocoa and then the children can catch us up on everything."

The thought of cocoa brightened Billy's mood. He loved the stuff. Bittersweet chocolate brewed with angel tears was one of his favorite treats, from back when he was a skeleton boy.

That was before Mum Biglum had become a world-renowned chocolatier, and when Billy's evil brother ruled High Manners Manor — the same brother who had locked Billy in the secrets-closet, starting a long otherworldly chain of events.

First, Billy's skeleton uncle, Grim, broke a good many Afterlife rules, when he changed Billy into a skeleton for the childless Mr. and Mrs. Bones. Then, years later, he broke a good many more by trying to dispatch Billy to the Afterlife. Uncle Grim had been attempting to cover his tracks because rumors of his first indiscretion had leaked out. But his plan backfired when Billy was transformed back into a living boy. A living boy, steeped in oddness, who was now in definite need of a good cuppa cocoa.

As Mrs. Bones clattered the cocoa service together, Billy looked around the closet. He was happy to see not much had changed, though there were fewer secrets trunks now.

As Mrs. Bones filled the pot with angel tears, Billy noticed a stack of secrets documents on the floor. *Strange,* he thought. Normally his parents had every document stamped, sorted, and tucked away in a secrets trunk moments after arriving in the closet.

Billy shuffled curiously through the pile as Millicent chatted with Mr. Bones.

Billy was about to place the documents back when one caught his eye. He slapped a hand to his mouth.

"What's that?" Millicent whispered.

"It's a secret," Billy said. He held up the document, dangling it like bait.

"And whose secret might it be?" Millicent asked.

"A very naughty girl's."

"Really."

"Oh yes. This naughty girl sneaks out at night to go swimming in the Codswattle. Oooooh, I don't think Mum Biglum would approve at all," Billy teased.

"Billy . . . don't you dare —," Millicent said. By now the conversation had moved well past whispers, capturing Mr. Bones's attention.

"Billy Bones Biglum! Put that down!" Mr. Bones commanded.

"And her name is Millicent Hues." Billy laughed.

"Billy!" Millicent and Mr. Bones shouted together.

The document leaped out of Billy's hand and blew apart — *BANG* — as secrets always do in the light of truth.

"That s-stings!" Millicent stammered.

"Errr. Sorry . . ."

"When are you going to learn how to keep a secret?" Millicent swatted away the ashes on her robe and gave him a sour look. Her expression softened a bit when she saw his embarrassment.

But Mr. Bones's face was hard as flint and sparks as he grabbed the stack of secrets out of Billy's hands. Before he could say anything, Mrs. Bones spoke up. "Lars Bones! Don't you go laying into him. You left those out, so this is no one's fault but your own!"

Billy hoped his skeleton parents weren't going to argue. Each time they did, he wanted to shrink through the cracks in the floorboards.

Mr. Bones walked stiffly to a trunk at the back of the closet. He flung it open, then sorted the secrets with his usual dispatch. He was muttering under his breath.

It sounded something like, "Fiddlesticks flotsam bother and bats!" But Billy really wasn't sure. The comments might have been much ruder.

Mr. Bones was calm by the time he returned. Then he did what any husband who's been successfully married to the same wife for over two hundred years would do. He sighed, "You're right, my dear."

Mrs. Bones went back to her cocoa and Mr. Bones continued, "However, that's not everything to be said about the incident. Is it, Billy?"

"No, sir," Billy admitted, shoulders sagging. "I shouldn't have poked around in your private stuff."

"Well, no real harm done. You've already apologized to Millicent, so we'll consider the case closed." Eyes dimming, Mr. Bones tilted his head. "I do wish I could have taught you how to hold a secret."

Mrs. Bones poured the cocoa. The children accepted their cups gladly, and after they all clinked cups in a toast, Billy excitedly caught them up on the visit to the ship.

"Of course the *Spurious II* won't be worth her salt unless she has the proper captain." Billy fidgeted with his teacup handle, then asked, "Can you help us get this message to Gramps Pete? We want him to come with us."

Mrs. Bones stirred her cocoa nervously and looked at her husband. Frowning, Mr. Bones took the note, turning it over in his hands a few times. "I'm sure Pete would make the grandest captain on the seven seas, six times over. But there are things going on in the Afterlife that will make it difficult to contact him." He lowered his voice. "Unfortunately, the Investigative Branch has been monitoring the mail — they have eyeballs everywhere — so it wouldn't do to pop off a note to their most wanted ghost." He dropped it onto a small pile of unsorted documents. "Best we keep it here. For some reason, they've linked Pete to Commissioner Pickerel's disappearance!"

Billy's heart skipped a beat. He glanced at Millicent. She shook her head in a warning.

Mr. Bones thumbed through the *Eternal Bugle* and then poked it with a bony finger. "Here's an article from earlier this week:"

New Afterlife Restrictions
by Headley B. Moan

Bugle readers may remember how Commissioner Pickerel nearly cornered the market on Afterlife

power last year. But his sudden disappearance left
his assistant, Miss Cornelia Chippendale, in charge.

Many souls are worried about new Afterlife
government restrictions. Bartemis Brittleback, chief
spokesman for the Skeleton Guild, said, "You so
much as jiggle your jawbone and you're shipped off
to Nevermore."

Bugle reporters tried to reach Mr. Brittleback
for additional comments, but he was unavailable.
When asked, Temporary Commissioner Cornelia
Chippendale said, "We don't know where he is, and
we will continue to not know where he is for a very
long time."

Emergency spying has been deemed necessary
to aid in the search for Glass-Eyed Pete. The
Investigative Branch has reason to believe he was
responsible for Commissioner Pickerel's mysterious
disappearance. "We strongly recommend that he get
in touch, or else!" said Temporary Commissioner
Chippendale.

Millicent's cup rattled on its saucer. "Are my parents
all right?" she asked after Mr. Bones stopped reading.

"They were when Mr. Benders ran a letter for them

two weeks ago." Mr. Bones answered, trying to look hopeful. "Unfortunately, he lost track of them last week."

Millicent sagged like a lost sock. Billy wasn't feeling much better. Trapping Pickerel obviously had unloosened a wobbly cart of events that was careening down a dangerous road.

"And what about both of you?" Billy asked his parents. "Will the Investigative Branch come after you again?"

"I think they've learned their lesson there." Mrs. Bones leaned over and patted Billy's hand, then retrieved his cup.

But Billy wasn't convinced. His skeleton parents had once been prisoners of Nevermore. They'd still be there too if he, Millicent, and Gramps Pete hadn't proved that the couple had been arrested illegally and then captured Pickerel for added insurance. It was nearly unheard of for anyone to be released from the dreadful place, and exceedingly unlikely anyone would be again.

Mr. Bones consulted his pocket watch and then his wife. "These two heroes really should get back to bed, my dear!" He slipped his watch into his vest then followed Mrs. Bones and the children to the door.

"Hopefully, children," Mrs. Bones said, "next time, we'll have much better news."

There was nothing Billy wanted more. He wished his parents' bony embraces could squeeze away all of his concerns.

Outside the secrets-closet, a scarlet shape snaked away from the keyhole. It dimmed its glow until the children passed, and then the manifestation silently inched along, hungry to hear what delicious new secrets they were keeping.

Billy and Millicent left the secret passageway through an equally secret door set in the dining room wall and continued toward their bedrooms.

"I'm worried, Billy."

Billy's eyes narrowed. "We've got to do something, Mill. It's all my fault."

"Should we tell your parents?"

Billy stopped at the base of a winding staircase. "I

don't know. . . ." His words echoed through the grand hallway. The crystal chandeliers tinkled with icy indifference.

Billy flumped onto the steps.

Millicent sat next to him. "We've got to have a plan."

"Well, we know someone powerful who's back and forth between the two worlds every day."

"Your Uncle Grim?"

"He *did* help out before. The trick is to get in touch." Billy looked skyward.

Millicent got up and walked absentmindedly in a small circle. A few muttering moments later she smiled. "I know a way. Think about it. What's your uncle's job?"

"Hall of Reception's chief field agent. When people die, he escorts their souls to the Afterlife."

"Well there you have it, then."

"Have what?"

"The answer, Billy." Millicent cocked her head. "If we want to find Uncle Grim, all we have to do is wait near someone who is about to pass away. Then Uncle Grim is bound to show up."

"How do we do that?"

Millicent tilted her head more, until her exasperation looked like it would leak out of her ear.

"Martha's uncle!" Billy jumped up.

Millicent nodded. "Yes, but let me handle it."

"I'll stay quiet as a bug's breath."

"You better."

The children continued up the stairs, echoes of their voices skipping like pond stones and then sinking with a wobble into the darkness.

A scarlet glow brightened at the base of the stairs, and Gossip's snaky shape expanded.

Finally, sssomething worth sharing!

The manifestation drew the curtains separating this world from the next, and slithered through the shimmering hole.

Chapter 3

Temporary Commissioner Chippendale

Miss Cornelia Chippendale could have had any style of office she wanted: a Renaissance cathedral, faceted diamonds and pearls, or a life-sized da Vinci mural. But Miss Chippendale preferred the look of ancient Egypt.

When Pickerel disappeared, she moved into his old office and brought along her temple: every glassy gold tile, sandstone block, column, and flickering torch sconce.

Miss Chippendale smiled at her hunky servants. They fanned her with ostrich plumes, fed her bonbons, and massaged her feet with sweet-smelling oils. Since taking over for Commissioner Pickerel, Miss Chippendale had gained almost as much weight as power. Her robes were tight as an apple skin. With slashing strokes of her steel-nib pen, she dashed off her signature on a tall stack of documents hovering in the air.

"Your ten o'clock appointment has arrived, madam,"

Mr. Panderglass, her young assistant, informed her. Despite his handsome features, he looked tired. Miss Chippendale's growing rank had made him a very busy man.

"Oh yes . . . I'd quite forgotten."

Mr. Panderglass bowed and disappeared as Gossip, her loyal snoop, slithered in.

Miss Chippendale smiled politely. "So good to see you, my friend."

Gossip glided through the air toward the dais, moving with the grace of a python. Miss Chippendale conjured up a smaller version of her own throne and Gossip gratefully curled up among its purple silk cushions.

"Ssso good to sssee you, too, my dear," Gossip hissed in a voice swirling with empty echoes and whistling wind. "Not to put businesss before pleassssantries, but I do have a bit of information."

Miss Chippendale briskly rubbed her palms. "My, my. But where are my manners?" She clapped her hands. A small assortment of teacakes appeared between the two thrones. A teapot poured itself into two fancy china cups. "Now, my friend, you were saying?"

The manifestation wasn't saying much. It was too busy stuffing its mouth and slurping tea. Miss Chippendale looked into her teacup. "I am most curious about what's brought you here today."

"Yesss, information you'll find essspecially comforting. I know how dedicated you were to your old bossss, Commissioner Pickerel."

"Quite." Miss Chippendale said, eyelids draped over a sideways glance.

The manifestation inched forward. "Usually, my information is free as the sssslither on a sssnake, but I've a price this time."

Miss Chippendale's smile dripped with faked concern. "Which is?"

"I'm not as fetching as I once wasss . . . I wouldn't mind a little refurbishing. . . ."

The temporary commissioner took a long sip, studying the manifestation like it was a pinned bug. Then she leaned forward, patting Gossip's hand. "My good, good friend, Gossip. You've been so helpful these last few years, I don't want you wasting one golden wish on restoring yourself. The Black Grotto Spa seems just the ticket. You'll be back to your old self in no time." She smiled graciously. "Stay as long as you like. And put it all on my account."

Gossip offered a simpering nod and recounted how Billy and Millicent trapped the commissioner with Pete's help, and shared their new plans to contact Grim.

Miss Chippendale was silent for a moment, her brows a single ominous stroke. Then she swung her arms overhead and clapped. Two servants appeared. Bowing crisply, they lifted Gossip onto a cushion. Before there was time to offer any thanks, they had already paraded Gossip out of the temple.

"Cheers, my dear. I'm sure you'll love every moment," Miss Chippendale called out, and when the doors banged closed she added, "in Nevermore."

Miss Chippendale sighed as she inspected the dazzling rings on her fingers. This boy, Billy, and that girl, Millicent: they had caused problems for the Investiga-

tive Branch before. And now it appeared they were behind Pickerel's disappearance. If they could trap the
commissioner, they could also choose to release him.
Miss Chippendale had grown to like her new job far too
much to let that happen.

Chapter 4
Uncle Mordecai

Billy's first opportunity to ask Martha about her uncle came the next morning. "Oooooh, but it's a gloomy morning. Looks like a storm's brewing," Martha said, sweeping open his curtains. "Certain as a nod bobs your noggin."

Billy hesitated.

After all, one doesn't usually ask, "Is your uncle going to die today?"— at least not first thing in the morning. Also, Billy had promised Millicent he'd wait for her. They needed a gentle way into the matter and would never dream of hurting their dear nanny's feelings.

Martha continued around the room, picking up carelessly dropped clothing. She stopped mid-bustle and stared at Billy. "I sent you to bed clean and now you're covered in dust."

"Sorry, Martha, I'm afraid I had an awful nightmare. I took a little walk."

"Oh you poor thing . . . I should have been up to help you. Had a sleepless night myself." Martha plucked at Billy's hair with a concerned squint.

A short time later, Billy, scrubbed spic-and-span, joined Millicent and Dame Biglum in the dining room. He was wearing navy blue shorts and a sailor shirt. Millicent had on a bright red corduroy jumper. The table was decked out with stacks of toast slicked gold with honey, platters of bacon, and several small mountains of pancakes.

After breakfast, Billy and Millicent looked for the right opening to ask Martha about her uncle. But it didn't come right away. She proceeded through her day in her typical sunny manner, and the children watched, hoping for even a frown. They peered over their books during reading hour; stared at her through the deep-sea aquarium while she fed the giant squids; spied while she sprinkled Brazil nuts for the macaws in the aviary; and they dropped more than a few notes during violin lessons. They were paying more attention to the clicks of Martha's heels than the metronome.

"Children!" Martha finally cried out. "You're crowding me so close, it feels like I got three sets of bums in my bloomers!"

"We've been worried about you, Martha," Millicent confessed. "Your poor uncle. How is he?"

Martha sighed. "Not well. Course it's hard to feel too sad for him. None of the family can stand him."

"He can't be *that* bad." Billy frowned. He couldn't imagine anyone related to Martha having even the smallest flaw.

"He's that bad and worse." Martha nodded regretfully. "Still, he needs help. It's a sad day when a whole family turns their back. I'm afraid, children, that's what really got me so glum." Martha sniffed.

Millicent glanced at Billy. "Maybe we can do something?" she suggested.

Martha's eyes glistened. "I should have known you two dear hearts would lend a hand."

"We should visit him straightaway, don't you think?" Billy insisted. "It might help him feel better."

"I suppose so, lambs." Martha dabbed her eyes and then tucked her hanky into her sleeve. "But it won't be pleasant, I can promise you. Sure you still want to go?"

Both children nodded.

Dame Biglum was quick to allow this visit, so Billy, Millicent, and Martha threw on their raincoats and went out into the gathering gloom.

Mr. Colter, the coachman, drew the carriage to the front of the manor. The children clambered up and wedged in next to Martha. Mr. Colter nodded to his passengers, and when his gaze got round to Martha, he blushed. Martha's cheeks were red, too — the brightest things going on this dreary day.

Billy watched the two adults, baffled by their behavior, but Millicent wore a quiet smile.

In a half hour's time, the carriage drove down into a small valley. Stonehamm was a most appropriate name for the rock-strewn fields and misshaped cottage.

The children followed Martha as she stepped up the fieldstone stoop. She knocked timidly on the front door, then knocked harder. When no one responded, she sighed and let them all in.

There was a secrets-closet at Stonehamm Farm cottage, as there is everywhere people call home, tucked into the shadows behind a wardrobe. Unlike the Boneses' snug closet, here, trunks were overflowing, their documents scattered everywhere. Among the mess lay the snoring Liam Slackbones, skeleton master of this run-down outpost.

For the last few days Slackbones had been celebrating the imminent arrival of Grim and the departure of Uncle Mordecai's soul. But most of all, he looked forward to a nice holiday without the responsibility of looking after Uncle Mordecai's lies.

Liam Slackbones slept through the sharp knock at the front door.

The front door complained loudly as Martha and the children stepped inside.

The dark cottage smelled of wood rot. Martha's nose wrinkled as she lit a runty candle, then lifted it high. The room contained only a few sticks of rough-hewed furniture. Flies circled the unwashed bowls overturned on the table.

The children held on to Martha's skirts as they crossed to the bedroom door. The room contained an old wardrobe and bed — both poorly made, as if the carpenters had thrown their lumber together and fled. A few heart thumps later, they noticed a gnarled old man in bed. His eyes were closed. He held a dry bean clamped between his finger and thumb.

Martha brought the candle to her uncle's face and gasped. "Looks like we're too late, children. Uncle Mordecai has passed on." She lowered the candle and her voice.

She stood, head bowed in respect, then reached down with her free hand and drew a grubby gray sheet over the old man's body. But as she was about to cover his head, his eyes snapped open. They were yellow as runny yoke.

Martha shrieked.

"Trying to take my last bean!" His voice was gravelly as his barren fields. "I know you are. But I'll take it to the grave with me!"

Martha whipped the candle back. Uncle Mordecai's glare narrowed. "And you want my farm, I'm thinkin'. Well, too late for that. I've locked the deed away. No one gets it," he finished, chest heaving in a rough coughing fit.

Billy frowned and stepped forward. "That's a nasty way to talk to our Martha."

Millicent was right behind him. "You should apologize."

Martha gasped. The vicious light in Uncle Mordecai's eyes bore in on Billy. Then he snapped a gnarled hand around the boy's neck. Billy's eyes nearly popped from his head as Uncle Mordecai dragged him toward his flinty shard of a nose. Millicent screamed and lunged forward, aiming to pry open the old man's grip.

Billy recoiled with shock. His bones glowed bright beneath his flesh as dark sparks danced around his body.

Uncle Mordecai's hand dropped. His eyes rolled up. And in that instant — in the tiny gap between a tick and a tock — everything froze:

Martha's candle locked in flickerless flame. A shout of warning stuck to her lips.

Millicent hung in the air, caught in the midst of her rush to save Billy.

Chapter 5

Shadewick Gloom

Anyone who spends time in the Afterlife is sure to see Government Hall spanning high overhead. And those who travel the length of this great corridor will notice that one end of the building looks much like the other. Light Side or Dark: polished stone floors lined with offices stretch to forever. But on the Dark Side, the lights are set lower and the heat is set much higher.

Around one particularly dark bend was the office of Shadewick Gloom. His title was Ambassador for the Department of Injustice. Which meant he was an exceedingly powerful Dark Side muckamuck.

Gloom had not always worked for the Dark Side. Not so long ago, he held high office on the Light Side. Only one other Afterlifer had ever moved to the Dark Side from the Light — the fellow who runs the place. Both had fallen from grace, but one had fallen much farther — all the way to the Lower Realms.

Higher beings rule the Afterlife from the Realms Above, but they do give a certain amount of autonomy to the Dark Side. They put lower beings in charge of Lower Realms, so they don't have to get their hands too dirty, and there's none as low as the big boss himself.

Shadewick's story was not as well known.

Except by Uncle Grim.

Shadewick Gloom used to escort souls to the Hall of Reception, everyone's first stop in the Afterlife. For years, Grim had served as Gloom's apprentice. But Shadewick truly enjoyed his time as the Grim Reaper, far more than he was supposed to. He had collected souls before they were due, and hid them for his own dark purposes. Which is why he'd created Nevermore.

How he created the place was another matter.

Years before Shadewick Gloom had been an exceptional student at Miss Spinetip's School for Secrets-Keeping Skeletons. Any skeleton who is anyone studies there. Uncle Grim was one of Miss Spinetip's stars. But no one could outshine Gloom's ability in shadow stretching.

Working with shadows has always been a specialty among skeletons. They discovered a way of opening shadows using skeleton keys. Then they stretched them to create secrets-closets — a handy way to hide from the living.

Gloom really pushed the envelope when he discovered how to weave shadows together in an endless chain, using nightmares. He kept that bit of business to himself, though, as he stitched together every shadow in the Afterlife and created Nevermore.

To get back and forth to his private world, he fabricated a spidery network of shadow tunnels. They could take him wherever he liked, so long as he remembered his key. There were only two of these extraordinary keys in the entire universe.

But Gloom's breakthrough left him with an unquenchable thirst for nightmares, and since then he hadn't been shy about collecting them.

This secret undertaking really took off after Commissioner Pickerel stumbled onto it. Soon, Nevermore became Pickerel's favorite dumping ground. It was a convenient way to get rid of misfits while avoiding a complicated court system. Pickerel took great care to never let on he was working with Gloom — that would have been frowned on, indeed. Even on the Dark Side.

When Grim found out about Nevermore, he raised the alarm. Shortly after, the High Council packed

Shadewick off to the Dark Side. But there he flourished even more. The Council may have stripped him of his position, but they couldn't take his ability. And he'd been gaining in strength ever since by mastering dark powers.

In all his splendiferous Dark Side surroundings, Shadewick's most prized possession was his bell jar collection. The glass domes contained the heads of his enemies. He displayed them proudly throughout his palace and loved examining them.

That's what Shadewick was doing when Hammer and Tongs rounded past him and then bounded down the hall. The shadow hounds were the size of Great Danes and black as dark intentions — the same shade as the robes shrouding Shadewick Gloom.

"Curious," he murmured, following after them, his murky cloak wafting behind.

Just then, he heard Miss Chippendale shouting. "Ohhhh, you great lummoxes. Get off!"

Shadewick entered the laboratory he affectionately called his "darkroom." Miss Chippendale lay sprawled on the floor as the two beasts licked her with slobbering tongues. Despite her high rank, Miss Chippendale couldn't wish herself into the Dark Side. Even if she had been able to, she didn't fancy leaving a financial paper trail by spending a golden wish. Gloom's web of shadowports was a cheaper way to travel, and a safer way of getting around the convoluted terrain of the Dark Side.

"Off!" Gloom snapped. The hounds backed away, tails drooping as they cowered behind their master. He helped the temporary commissioner onto her feet. "Cornelia Chippendale. This is a surprise. To what do I owe the pleasure?"

She hastily rearranged her cloak. "A favor among professionals, Mr. Ambassador."

"Why so formal?" He glanced sideways at the

twirling shadowport from which she had emerged and then back at his roundish guest. "You obviously feel comfortable enough to let yourself in. I gather you found Pickerel's key amongst his private papers. Were you snooping?"

Indeed Chippendale had been, the minute she suspected Pickerel was lost. She had also found many secrets along with the key. The kind of secrets one can use against one's enemies. She tried to cover her blush with a froglike "Harrumph!" but Gloom saw her twinge.

"Now, now, nothing to feel bad about. I do like snoops. Please call me Shadewick. Or better yet, Gloomy. That's what my nastiest friends call me."

Miss Chippendale blanched. "I'm here strictly on business." She glanced around suspiciously and then she pulled her hood over her head. "I prefer to make this quick. I have a proposition for you."

Gloom folded his arms.

"How would you like your old position back?"

Shadewick Gloom frowned. "I can only think of two things that would stand in the way of that. One is the Moral Authority's High Council."

"No worries there. As head of the Investigative Branch, I can take care of them."

Shadewick circled around her, rubbing his fingertips together. "My goodness, you've grown powerful. The other obstacle would be my old apprentice, Grim Bones."

Miss Chippendale's smile was thin as a sliver. "There you have it. You get rid of him, and you will have your full rank back, plus all those other benefits you're hungry for. I shall be glad to look the other way, so long as you're discreet."

Shadewick chuckled. "Well, hasn't this day turned ducky!"

"Uhm, there are only two other tiny matters beyond taking care of Grim Bones." Miss Chippendale clasped her hands behind her back.

Again, Gloom waited.

Chippendale's effort at a casual smile shook her double chins. "I need two children brought over to the Afterlife. You can do whatever you'd like with them, so long as they disappear."

Chapter 6
A Departing Soul

Time had stopped.

Billy knew only one hand that held that kind of power: Uncle Grim's. He'd been granted that ability to help him with the impossible task of being in too many places in too short a time.

Suspended seconds later, a stallion with a starlight mane galloped through the tumble-down cottage wall. It was Fleggs, and the heroic skeleton sitting astride was Uncle Grim. The skeleton reined the horse to a stop. He wore his usual Cloak of Doom, and the grin of an uncle very happy to see his nephew. Grim's bones danced with the same blue glow and black sparks of energy that had lit Billy up moments before.

As he dismounted, he said, "My boy, it's so good to see you — quite unexpected, though." Grim clapped a black-gloved hand on Billy's shoulder. "You're looking very healthy." His eyes crinkled in a deeper smile.

Martha and Millicent were bathed in the glow that danced between Billy and his uncle. *The plan worked,* Billy thought, *but Millicent's going to fuss about missing the excitement.*

Uncle Grim reached around Billy to pluck a dim orb out of Mordecai's chest. Most souls glow with color, but this one was drab as sandstone. Grim flicked the ball into the air, transforming it into a ghostly version of the old man. But before it floated back down to the bed, Billy started in, "I trapped Pickerel. He's in the magical vase. Now they're after Pete and maybe Millicent's parents, and —"

"Slow down, my boy. I can keep time stopped — there's no hurry." Interlocking his fingers at his waist, he gave Billy his full attention.

Billy led Grim through the story, one tangle at a time. When he was finished, Grim's expression matched his name. "I'm afraid we'll have to sort this out straightaway. Too many Afterlifers are paying for Pickerel's disappearance."

Billy looked away.

With a gentle caress to the chin, Grim turned Billy's head to face him. "Don't worry, you did right to trap Pickerel, and you're doing right by telling me now." He guided the boy away from the bed. "The best thing to do would be to tell my boss, Oversecretary Under-hill. He's a member of the Moral Authority's High Council."

Seeming to remember why he'd come in the first place, Grim glanced over his shoulder. Mordecai's spirit had gotten out of bed and was drifting across the room. "Oh bother," muttered Grim. Dark sparks of eternal energy trailed off his twirling finger, and an iridescent circle opened in the air. Grim floated the ghost toward the hole. Gripping the tunnel's edge, the old man grumpily dropped through. The hole closed with a small burp as if it had digested something unsavory.

Fleggs trotted over to nuzzle Billy. He had always been able to recognize the boy, body or bones.

"There's another matter we must face up to." Grim smiled but his voice was stern.

Billy looked up.

"When I arrived, time had already stopped."

"Collywobbles! How?" Billy gasped.

Grim took Fleggs by the halter. "I've long suspected you absorbed some of my powers when you turned from a skeleton back into a boy. I'm afraid that's against quite a few Afterlife rules. So it's past time I told Oversecretary Underhill about that, too. Even the angel of death is bound by regulations, my boy."

Billy's mouth dropped open. "But . . . does that mean you'll get shipped off to Nevermore?"

Grim drew the boy close. "Not if I can help it."

A cold sensation swept through Billy when Grim's cloak grazed him.

"Oversecretary Underhill is a first-rate skeleton and a solid friend. He and I think the time for secret prisons and Afterlife spying is over," Grim said. "The Investigative Branch has too much control."

Billy bit his lip. "They're horrible."

Grim leaned down and looked Billy in the eye. "Truth is, they *think* they're doing right. But don't worry, we'll set things straight. Right eventually flowers even out of the darkest wrong."

Despite Grim's grin, Billy felt unsettled. Lately, the adults around him had been awfully quick with assurances over things they couldn't control.

Uncle Grim stood, the hem of his cloak sweeping a trail of frost across the floor. Billy watched him swing into his saddle, then felt a scorching blast from behind.

A voice pierced the room like shards of dark crystal. "And that, my old assistant, will only happen over my smashed bones."

Shadewick Gloom stepped out of a whirling hole with his two huge shadow hounds snarling at his side.

Chapter 7
The Boneyard

Sad to say, but not every part of the Light Side is nice. Take Edgeton, for example. It's gray, dreary, and slop-full of dilapidation. That is because of its unfavorable location: next to the Dark Side. This sorry district is reserved for the lowest rungs of society, namely skeletons, and ghostly fugitives like Glass-Eyed Pete.

Pete had sought shelter in this shabby corner of the Afterlife now that Chippendale's spying eyeballs were everywhere. At the moment, he was lying low in the Boneyard, a rustic pub, filled with smells like oiled wood and pipe smoke.

Minnie Lumbus sat behind the backroom bar, tossing an occasional smile toward Pete. She was plump for a skeleton. *Large boned* she would say — all the better to wrap her guests in bone-crunching hugs when they needed them. Widow Lumbus had known Glass-Eyed

Pete for many years, and second to High Manners Manor, the tavern was his favorite haunt.

Pete looked splendid in his translucent blue coat. It was double buttoned with wide lapels and hung down to the tops of his buccaneer boots. Despite the softness of his ghostly glow, his face was wrinkled as a mummy's wink, but rarely wore a frown. Jenkins, his parrot, sat on his shoulder — a jewel-like green to Pete's filmy blue.

Pete scanned the two rogues who faced him with his glass eye. It was believed the eye was magic and helped him judge the souls of others. "Lads, thank ye for comin' by at such an early hour. An hour too early from the look of ye."

"Too right." Ned — Mrs. Lumbus's grown son — clattered in agreement. He was a hulking fellow with a battered jawbone, who wore the red cloak and silver emblem of a Skeleton Guide. It was his job to escort condemned souls to the Dark Side.

"This might make it worth yer while." Pete materialized a golden coin. It turned and floated within the gentle column of his pipe smoke. "One hundred golden wishes to both of ye, if ye can help me." Pete palmed the coin before anyone could grab it.

"Where'd you come across that, Pete?" Ned's chair creaked as he leaned forward. "The most you've had in your pockets before's been a hungering moth."

Pete took a steady pull of his pipe. "My friend will be bringing the rest of the loot soon." His good eye crinkled like salty sail canvas. "But with the gold comes a mission, lads."

"I've a bad feeling about this." Ned sighed.

"One hundred in gold can go a long way in calming our fear." This smooth voice belonged to Roger Jolly. He was a bit of a dandy by skeleton standards, wearing a tattered tailed suit and a top hat. Unlike most skeletons, Roger Jolly had hair. He wore it long, black, and sleek.

Pete exhaled a smoke plume. It circled the table and

then drifted apart. "Very well, me buckos, let's get down to business."

The skeletons leaned toward Pete — Ned on his ham-sized fists and Roger on an elegant elbow. Pete paused for dramatic effect, but the air was already thick with curiosity. "Here it is, lads." He spread his hands on the table. "How do ye get me into Nevermore? And *more* importantly, how do ye get me back out?"

Chapter 8
When Time Stands Still

Regretfully for skeleton historians, the Battle at Stonehamm Cottage lasted only seconds. Billy was pinned to the ground near Uncle Mordecai's bed when Shadewick Gloom and his snarling hounds sprang from their shadowport. From there, all Billy could see were two crackling bolts of purple light. The cottage shook with a thunderous explosion, then went quiet.

"Off!" Shadewick Gloom snapped.

The dogs obeyed instantly and Billy got his first clear look at the shadow-cloaked skeleton. There was something in his hands: *Uncle Grim's head!* Billy jumped to his feet. His eyes swept the room in a panic. Grim's headless body lay still, on the far side of the room.

As Fleggs reared up and whinnied, relief surged though Billy. The huge warhorse would surely set things straight. Fleggs pawed and snorted as he edged toward Shadewick, his eyes the color of spitting lava.

"Get him, Fleggs!" Billy cried.

Gloom held up Uncle Grim's head. "I'll smash it if you plant one hoof closer," he shouted.

Fleggs stopped.

Billy couldn't believe it. Could this dark skeleton win so easily?

Gloom lifted the skull. "Ah, poor Grim Bones." He snickered, then tucked the skull into the crook of his arm. He turned on Billy. "I expected some trickiness, but this is most unusual." He circled the boy slowly. "How is it that a human boy is still moving even though time has stopped? Hmmm. We'll have plenty of time to sort it out it because you're coming with me! But, first . . ." Shadewick strode toward Millicent.

"Noooo!" Billy swiped at his friend's arm, but the hounds pressed him back.

That voice. And this shrouded skeleton, they were straight out of his nightmares.

Shadewick Gloom smirked. He waved a hand toward Millicent's chest and out leaped a bright purple orb. A chill crept through Billy, frosting him to the bones.

Shadewick Gloom floated Millicent's glowing soul above his fingertips. "Delightful," he mused.

He didn't notice Grim's eyes light up. But Billy did. Uncle Grim was coming around!

Shadewick slunk toward Billy as the hounds took up a new post in front of Fleggs. "And now for you." He flexed his fingers like he was trying to choose melons in a grocer's bin. "Another ripe soul for Nevermore."

Billy leaped back, tripping over the bed.

"Hold still, boy." Gloom raked Billy's chest with sharp fingertips.

The touch burned and the room whirled. Out of the dimness, he heard Grim shout, "Pull, Billy! You've done it before!"

Blue glows and black sparks flared around Billy. In a flash, he was more bones than body. Eternal energy twisted out of his chest and up his arms. Shadewick reached for the bright blue ball of Billy's soul. But the boy reached out and pulled back.

By then, Grim's headless body was back on its feet. It took a menacing step forward. Fleggs rumbled back into the fray. Hammer and Tongs lunged at the horse's flanks, but the huge beast was too powerful.

Shadewick Gloom saw which way the tide of battle was turning. He retreated, uttering a string of the Dark Side's least delicate curses. With Millicent's soul and Grim's head in hand, he stepped back into his shadowport. Hammer shot through next, the victim of Fleggs's powerful fetlock. And a yelping Tongs swiftly followed.

Billy lunged after them, but it was too late. The shadowport was nearly closed. Billy caught Grim's last shout —"The Boneyard!"— before the hole twisted shut.

In the dim light of Stonehamm Cottage, Billy was left with Martha, still as a headstone; Grim's headless body fumbling around on the floor; and his best friend's soulless body, frozen in time, reaching out to save him.

Chapter 9
Timelessness Marches On

The last time Millicent felt like this, she had been a passenger in Professor Dabbleton's rocket-powered dirigible. Too much kick in his thrusters and she had found herself a thousand feet in the air, swearing her stomach was a thousand feet below.

A horrid skeleton was leading her through a spiraling hall. *Am I dead?* she wondered. But her stomach felt too topsy-turvy to believe that. It was a most unusual sensation, like she wasn't altogether there.

A purple glow scuffed the edges of the walls. It took Millicent a moment to realize the light was coming from her. She looked down at her arms and legs. They were as ghostly as Glass-Eyed Pete! Then she saw something worse. The skeleton in front of her was carrying Uncle Grim's head. Grim was scowling.

And as if all this wasn't enough, two shadowy hounds loped ahead — each leaving a wake of sludge.

It was all most curious.

Eventually, they stepped into a cavernous room, filled with lenses, crystal globes, prisms, surveying instruments, and even several orreries. *It's some kind of laboratory,* Millicent thought. But for what kind of strange science?

The skeleton slammed Uncle Grim's head next to a lens the size of a globe. He turned to one of his hounds. "Take her into the next room, Tongs. But don't let her drift away. Hammer, you wait by the shadowport."

Both dogs obeyed. Tongs gripped Millicent by her dress and trotted her into the hallway. She floated behind with as much ability to resist as a balloon. From its scowl, Millicent guessed the dog wasn't fond of light.

Tongs released her, then flopped next to the door. She drifted toward the center of the room and circled slowly. Many children would have died of fright by now, but not Millicent. She lived for these kinds of mysteries. She was scared, of course. But with measured steps and trembling breaths, she regrouped and looked around.

She was in a kitchen. Thick wooden islands were chockablock with ingredients in large glass jars. Bits and pieces of body parts wriggled inside each one. A handful of eyeballs blinked at her. Millicent shuddered.

When she tried to take a step away, she sank partway through the floor, then sprang into the air again. After numerous attempts, one thing was certain. Running away was out of the question.

Millicent drifted as close as she dared to the door, until the hound growled a low warning. She could hear snips of the conversation in the next room. The shadow skeleton's voice carried particularly well.

"Now, now, Grim. My dear ex-assistant. Don't be such a sourpuss. You are to be the crown jewel of my collection. The least you could do is show off that big skeleton smile."

Who is that beastly skeleton? Millicent wondered.

"I'll smile, Shadewick, when you're locked up thirteen levels below," she heard Uncle Grim croak.

Ah! Millicent tucked the name away.

"Not much chance of that, old thing. You see, I'm on the best of terms with the One below. Besides, no one will hear you when I put this jar over your head." Millicent heard the ring of a glass bell. Shadewick must have tinged the glass with a fingertip. The shadow skeleton continued. "It's quite soundproof. You won't be able to call your nasty horse."

"Be glad I can't. He'd splinter your body —"

All Millicent could hear from Uncle Grim after that were muffled curses. She turned toward the farthest wall, but this whole walking business was like trying to get around on a lake bottom.

Millicent heard Shadewick chuckle right behind her. She turned to see him pull a key from a shadowy sleeve. It had a scrollwork horse head for a handle and the shaft ended in a large crystal eyeball, filled with radiant black energy.

Shadewick studied Millicent's face. "You have a most familiar look." He stroked the key with sharp fingertips. The sound raised her neck hairs. "Ah, yes . . . I know who you are. I shall station you next to your parents. That should be lovely, I'm sure."

Chapter 10
Billy's New Bones

Slowly, with a few prods from Fleggs, Billy sat up. He still felt horrid as hag's breath, but had to do something. Millicent would have. "Get your teacup out of its saucer and get busy!" he could imagine her saying.

As Billy dragged himself up, Grim's headless body bumped into him. It was holding a creased sheet of paper in one hand and swirling the other in a gesture of writing.

He wants a pen!

Billy grabbed the candle from Martha's hand, the flame still frozen in mid-flicker. He searched the cottage, lighting up every dank corner until finally stumbling across a crumpled grocery list and a pen.

He darted back to the bedroom, then, steering Grim's body to the bed, he placed the writing instrument in its hands. It took a number of scribbling strokes before the body figured out how to produce something legible. Billy read the offered note, his knees shakier than the handwriting.

Billy, not sure how long I can keep time stopped . . . still possible to save Millicent. Ride Fleggs to the Afterlife! If time restarts, Millicent will be lost forever in Shadewick Gloom's hideaway, Nevermore!

Go to the Boneyard. Get help. Can't write more. He's coming this way . . . I fear he's going to —

Grim's pen clattered to the floor. His body twitched and bent over — hands contorted like claws, arms crossed and shaking.

Billy felt horrible leaving Grim, but staying couldn't help his uncle and would only put Millicent into more danger. He jammed the note in his raincoat pocket, and then, scraping a chair alongside Fleggs, he clambered aboard.

On any normal day (if there was such a thing in this odd boy's life), Billy would have banged off a stout little jig. Second to pirating, a ride on Fleggs was his favorite thing. Instead, Billy shouted and snapped the reins, "Come on Fleggs. Uncle Grim wants you to take me to the Boneyard!"

Billy pulled the reins tight to his chest, leaned into the horse's starry mane, and closed his eyes. He held on for dear life — Millicent's dear life.

Chapter 11

By the Grace of Minnie's Knuckles

For a jaw-dropping moment, there was silence at the Boneyard table. Then the skeletons reacted.

"Help you get to *Nevermore?*" Ned Lumbus blustered. "Pete, your brain's a mile wide of its berth!"

Roger only stared, but his eyes were cold as cod scales as they took the measure of the old pirate.

"Look, Pete," Ned said. "Most in the Afterlife have heard about the place, but no one knows where it is. I have grave doubts it's even on the Dark Side."

Pete aimed his pipe stem at the burly skeleton. "It's got to be."

"But it's not." Roger Jolly slipped his legs off the table. His boots landed with two smart *whaps*. "If you like, I can tell you where it is, and who's in charge."

Ned looked at him like his brain was as fogbound as Pete's.

"Thing is"— Roger hinged his fingers open and extended a palm toward Pete —"I need to see all hundred wishes before I say another word."

Pete dropped back in his chair, massaging his stubbly chin. His parrot, Jenkins, struck a matching pose. "My friend usually arrives well before anyone's ready to see him. I can't imagine what's keeping him."

With a clatter of sparking hooves, Billy and Fleggs arrived outside the Boneyard. The whoosh from their entrance swung the tavern sign. It was handpainted, depicting a graveyard with skeleton arms sticking out of its plots. They were holding beer mugs, raised in a foamy toast.

Billy looked around as the sign creaked to a stop. The street was empty as a headless man's hat and the Boneyard looked closed for business. Not a light flickered inside. *Now what?*

Billy swung off his saddle and dropped to the cobblestones. The resulting clatter led him to an important discovery. He held up a bony hand, flexing his fingers. *I'm a skeleton again!*

As Billy stood goggling, Fleggs nosed the boy's

pocket. After a few more luminous eye blinks, Billy took the hint. He pulled out Grim's note, noticing the unusual fold. Typically a note-writer folds the paper to conceal its contents. But his uncle had written on the outside (a very un-noteworthy thing to do).

Billy shook the folds open and discovered someone else's message inside:

Grim,

Aye, I'll be happy to help ye with yer task. As ye might guess, I'd like nothing more than to clear me name.

Meet me at the Boneyard Tavern in Edgeton. Find Minnie Lumbus. I told her to expect an awesome powerful bloke. She'll lead ye to me. And don't forget the bag of wishes. I'll need every ounce of gold.

Thank Cecil Benders for me for takin' this note to ye.

Hope surged in Billy as he checked over the note again. *Grim must have been on his way to the Boneyard to meet Gramps Pete! But what about the golden wishes? And* just as if Billy had spent a golden wish to find out, Fleggs turned to leave, jingling with every step.

"Hang on, Fleggs," Billy called as he grabbed the horse's halter.

After a quick clamber up to the saddlebags and an even quicker one down, Billy held a purple silk sack bound tight by a gold drawstring. It was fat with golden wishes.

Fleggs nickered. It sounded like a soft chuckle. Then with more sparks and clatters, but significantly fewer jingles, Fleggs shot through the fog and vanished.

Billy wondered where he could hide the gold and then remembered one of the great advantages of being a skeleton. An empty ribcage is a wonderful place to stash your loot. Gold secured, he bounded toward the tavern door.

Hammer slammers! I hope this thing is open! He whipped up the steps, flinging the door open.

"Young man. Most people know not to come messing about in the Boneyard." Mrs. Lumbus cracked her large knuckles. She gave Billy the once-over. "Don't you have a pretty blue glow. Not very common for a skeleton."

"I'm here to see my great-many-greats grandfather Pete." Billy's grin flashed at the idea of seeing the old pirate again.

All warmth drained from Mrs. Lumbus's manner. She muttered, "He said to expect someone awesome powerful . . . Must be some kind of a trick."

"He's here, isn't he?"

"Nope. Not here." Mrs. Lumbus crossed her sturdy arms.

"He has to be!" Billy's jaw opened and closed as he struggled to think. How could he have failed Millicent so soon?

"I'm sorry to turn you out, young man, but you have no business being in here unaccompanied by an adult." She herded him toward the door. "I could lose my tavern license."

Billy clutched her arm. "But . . . I'm . . . trying to help Uncle Grim."

Mrs. Lumbus hesitated. "Grim Bones?"

Billy nodded.

"He *is* one who's awesome powerful." Mrs. Lumbus's eyes rekindled their kindness. "Follow me."

"Billy me boy, it's good to see ye!" Pete boomed when Mrs. Lumbus and the young visitor entered the back room.

Billy leaped into Pete's translucent arms and was rewarded with a wonderful squeeze. He wouldn't have traded it for eleven back-to-back birthday parties.

The skeletons fiddled with their pipes, watching the curious reunion as Mrs. Lumbus resumed her post, polishing mugs.

"I was expectin' someone else in yer place. Where's yer uncle?" Pete draped his arm around Billy's shoulder.

Pete's question reminded Billy there was no time to spare. He quickly explained the strange chain of events: the appearance of Shadewick Gloom, Millicent's kidnapping, and the loss of Grim's head. He finished with, "We've got to save Millicent and Uncle Grim from Shadewick Gloom!"

"Then that's just what we'll do, me boy." Pete trumpeted in his most captain-ly voice. "We're going after Shadewick Gloom!"

Jenkins pointed a pinfeather into the air and struck a heroic pose. "Awk! Get Gloom!"

"We're going nowhere 'til you show us some gold," Ned said.

Pete pressed closer to Billy. "Now, lad, I have to ask ye a rather delicate question. Much hangs in balance at yer answer."

Billy reached inside his raincoat and rummaged in his ribcage. Yanking out the sack of wishes, he emptied it onto the table and then smiled at the delight in Pete's eye as the coins jingled into a heap.

"Clever lad." Pete dragged up a nearby chair, making room for the boy at the table. Bathed in reflections of gold, the value of the skeletons' grins increased tenfold. Before they could sweep the coins into their pockets, Pete warned them, "The loot stays here, tucked snug in Minnie's lockbox 'til the job is done."

Ned studied Pete through thoughtful eyes and then turned to Roger. "He's right. There's not much to gain by traipsing through the Dark Side jingling like jim-dandy. It'll only draw attention."

"What about the boy?" Ned grumbled. "Problem is he knows too much. We can't leave him here, and we can't take him with us. He'll whimper like a baby at all the vicious doings and horrible creatures."

Billy jumped up. "I didn't come here so you'd leave me behind."

"He's good in a tussle and sneaky as a tick. Not that ye'd guess it by his face." Pete swelled his luminous chest. "He tangled against the Investigative Branch's finest and came out on top. I promise he won't disappoint ye."

Billy's cheekbones burned with embarrassment as Ned and Roger studied him with new respect. Those were sizable shoes Pete was describing. Billy wasn't sure if he could fill one of them, let alone two.

Chapter 12
Oversecretary Underhill

Cecil Benders clacked down the marble floor, limping with the weight of his mail bag. He weaved to avoid the other skeletons packing this section of Government Hall, then hobbled to a stop in front of an impressively large door.

A small brass plate read: LORD SAGACIOUS UNDERHILL, OVERSECRETARY OF THE HALL OF RECEPTION AND THE DEPARTMENT OF FIBS AND FABRICATIONS.

Once inside, Mr. Benders hurried toward a second large door. Behind it, muffled voices were raised in battle. The old courier had to leap out of the way as the door unexpectedly flew open.

Miss Chippendale stomped out. "We shall see what the High Council thinks of your stubbornness, Underhill!" she lashed out over her shoulder. "Grim Bones is not fit for duty, and I'll prove it!"

An elderly skeleton with a high forehead and

impressively large brow bones appeared at the door-
way. His purple-trimmed robe swished as he dipped a
small bow. "Always a pleasure, Cornelia."

Adjusting her gloves impatiently, Miss Chippendale
nearly knocked Mr. Benders off his feet. She bustled by,
nose high.

"Your pardon, miss." Mr. Benders lifted his cap.
"Nasty old cow," he hissed under his breath.

Re-shouldering his courier bag, he shuffled up to
Underhill.

The Oversecretary blinked pleasantly. "Cecil."

He ushered Mr. Benders into his office and sat him
on a marble bench. Rounding the desk, he tidied up a
few documents, then sat down opposite in a high-
backed stone chair. "Is this an official visit? Or just one
old friend brightening the day of another?"

For a moment, Mr. Benders drifted back to the days
they had served together in the skeleton cavalry —
those were exciting times.

But the thought of danger shook Mr. Benders back
to the present. "There's a situation at the Department
of Eternal Energy, Sagacious. The generators are slow-
ing down."

Mr. Benders dug the message out of his bag and

handed it over. Oversecretary Underhill tapped a bony finger on his chin as he read it.

"The engineers are always talking to us like we're children," Mr. Benders chattered. "There's two whole paragraphs explaining the history of existical energy and eternal energy — real basic stuff. It says how millions of years ago, when the first living thing died, it released the two magical energies: one that powers the magic of Earth and the other that powers the Afterlife. There's a bunch of blah, blah, blah technical stuff after that, but the upshot is that neither of these energies are being produced at the moment because nothing's dying. Seems a time stoppage on Earth is the cause."

"I should say!" The oversecretary sighed wearily — ignoring the fact that his old friend had been reading notes as well as delivering them that day. "It's clearly an unscheduled stoppage. Something must have happened to Grim Bones."

Mr. Benders fumbled with his bag as he placed it on the bench. It thudded on the floor, contents fluttering down just behind. Some of Grim's correspondence was scattered into the pile. The old courier bent over and hastily collected the mess, paying particular attention to one wax-sealed envelope. "I hope it doesn't have anything to do with this message to Glass-Eyed Pete."

The bulge of Underhill's frown looked like a rock ledge. "Glass-Eyed Pete is mixed up in this? This *is* an emergency," he said, fingering his silver medallion. "We must alert every secrets keeper on Earth to conduct a search for Grim Bones. I shall require a regiment of skeleton messengers within the next few minutes."

Oversecretary Underhill turned to Mr. Benders. "Your territory on Earth includes the Boneses, does it not?"

"It does."

"You're to start there." Underhill scribbled off a quick note and handed it to Mr. Benders.

Mr. Bones was reading his copy of the *Eternal Bugle* while Mrs. Bones flounced a feather duster around a cobwebbed trunk. Her duster clattered to the floor as Mr. Benders slammed open the secrets-closet door.

"Good heavens, man! What's the fuss?" Mr. Bones snapped.

Mr. Benders hobbled into the closet. "Time stopped and a field agent down is fuss enough, I should say!"

"An F.A.D.!" Mr. and Mrs. Bones repeated in two gasps. The trunk lid clunked noisily as Mrs. Bones sat down.

"Here, Lars." Mr. Benders handed Mr. Bones a sealed note. "I'm sure you'll have this sorted out in no time at all." He tried to sound calm as he rocked nervously on his creaky old feet.

The Boneses were regional leaders, in charge of emergency response. Mr. Bones doffed his trusty departmental hat. He slipped on his spectacles, and then, breaking the document's seal, he scanned the note. "It's from Oversecretary Underhill."

Mrs. Bones rushed to her husband's side to read over his shoulder.

My Dear Lars and Decette:

By now I'm sure that Cecil has informed you that we have a field agent down. And I needn't tell you that means Grim is in serious danger. Unfortunately, so is my position and the very future of the D.F.F. There's no telling how unstable this situation will become if the council gets word of an unscheduled time stoppage. A power outage caused by Grim and even a whiff of Pete will play right into Cornelia Chippendale's hands.

I am truly sorry that at a time I should be offering my deepest condolences I must urge you to action. But as two of my best, I know you will get this situation under control.

My deepest sympathy and unflagging support,

Sagacious Underhill

"Right, Cecil," Mr. Bones said as calmly as he could manage. "We'll meet the rest of the secrets keepers at the rendezvous point." But his hand bones trembled as he tucked the note into his vest pocket.

Mr. Benders instinctively swept up the outgoing mail. Neither rain nor sleet nor an Afterlife emergency would keep this skeleton from his appointed rounds. His hand paused when he spotted Billy's note to Pete sitting atop a nearby pile. "Don't want that mixed up with the rest of your mail."

"Celesdon's Bells! I'm getting fluff-headed. I meant to get rid of that."

Mr. Benders tucked the note into his bag. "Don't work yourself up too much, Lars. Special deliveries are my specialty. I have to stop later at the Boneyard anyhow." Turning gingerly, he limped out the door, leaving it open. "Best of luck, old friends. I'll be back to help as soon as I can." He hobbled next through a shimmering portal, and past the curtains that separate this world

from the next. With the proper Afterlife permissions, even a solid old skeleton like Mr. Benders could travel like a ghost.

Mr. and Mrs. Bones gathered up a map and a list of fellow closet skeletons. In no time they were crunching across the manor's gravel turnabout, between suspended raindrops. It would have been a stiff morning rain, had time not been stopped.

One good thing about dangerous situations — they can really focus your resources. And this one had Mr. Bones's energy level soaring like an emergency flair. In all the centuries he'd been dead, he never felt so alive!

Part 2

In the Shadow of Gloom

If you want to flee Gloom's shadow
it's easy as can be.
You need only cast your eyes about
and find a nightmare key.

Chapter 13

Nevermore

Shadewick Gloom yanked Millicent through the last of the shadow hallway and stepped into Nevermore. The place was maliciously dark, made colder by a starless sky.

Gloom led her down a broad set of stone steps, his hounds skulking beside him. Stretching in front of Millicent was a cemetery, extending into a vast city of twisted tombs. As Gloom hauled her through the narrow streets, she could hear a thin wash of screams — thousands, perhaps millions of them, drifting in the darkness. Knowing that two of the voices belonged to her parents made her translucent skin crawl.

How will I find them? The place is so impossibly big.

Shadewick clacked along, talking to his hounds. "You know, boys, I think we need a decorative touch just over there." He stopped and nibbled his thumb bone. "A five-story mausoleum would do the trick."

The hounds panted happily.

"SHADEWICK GLOOM!" a woman's voice bellowed, bouncing through the city's musty stonework.

Gloom's expression shriveled. "Cornelia Chippendale."

Millicent recognized the name from the *Eternal Bugle*, the paper Billy's parents always read. She strained to see the face of the woman who was after Gramps Pete.

A woman wrapped in a black cloak arrived in a waddling trot. "I sent you on a simple errand, Gloom, and you completely botched it."

"Now, how can you say that, Cornelia, my dear?" Shadewick Gloom feigned shock. "Grim Bones is out of commission, and I've this little dumpling in my possession, too." He swung Millicent over his shoulder, dangling her as proof.

Miss Chippendale reminded Millicent of a snake coiling for a strike. "Well, if you've done such a dandy job, WHERE'S THE BOY AND WHY HAS TIME STOPPED?!!"

"Now, Cornelia . . ."

"I've managed to lay the problem on Underhill's doorstep. Still! How could you let this happen?"

Underhill! Millicent thought. She had shared enough conversations with Billy to know Underhill was an im-

portant official in the Afterlife. And a good one, too: not like *this* creepy woman.

"And as you can plainly see," Chippendale continued, "the girl's not quite dead! Until you restart time, there's a chance she can get back to her body."

Thundering waves wouldn't have struck Millicent with more force. *I'm not dead yet!* This explained why she was still so ghostly in the Afterlife and why it felt like so much of her had been left behind. Her glow exploded like sunburst.

"Now look what you've done, Chippy," Gloom growled. "You've gone and given her hope." He shook Millicent like a dust rag.

Miss Chippendale stammered, "W-well . . . for pity's sake, put that girl in the darkest hole you can find!" Then a cunning smile crept onto her lips. "Or you might unleash a dread on her first."

From the way she said it, Millicent was certain she wasn't talking about a word that described fear, but something that inspired it.

"After that, GET THE BOY and anyone else that might have witnessed your bungling!" temporary Commissioner Chippendale shouted as she waddled back toward the shadowport. Then, digging for something inside her cloak, she withdrew a strange object — horse head on one end, eyeball on the other.

She has her own shadowport key! Millicent rubbed her forehead. *That means there must be a hallway leading to the Light Side. . . .* Millicent *had* to do something. The list of people in need of saving, herself included, was growing by the minute!

Chapter 14
At Edgeton's Edge

Not much had changed at the Boneyard. Roger took a long draw on his pipe. Smoke leaked from the sides of his jaws and though his nose and ear holes as he spoke. "Like I said. There is a way to get to Nevermore. The boy's already mentioned the one who can get you there." His eye drifted to Billy along with his pipe smoke.

Pete considered Roger through shrewd lids. "Shadewick Gloom? And how did ye come by such information?"

"The Jollys are well connected. Better than you might imagine. Real bluebloods we'd be, if we *had* any blood."

Ned leaned on one elbow, and then the other, then tapped fingers and toes. It appeared to Billy that Ned might have heard how terribly well connected the Jollys were a few times before.

Roger banged on. "Skeletons have always been good with shadows. Like the way we use them to place secrets-closets in houses short on storage space. But Gloom's experiments have taken shadows to places never dreamed possible. It didn't take much to figure out he was behind Nevermore."

"Busy man, Gloom," Ned said, impressed.

Roger cocked a look at his fellow skeleton. "Most people have no idea he used to work for the government."

"I knew that," Billy blurted. "My Uncle Grim used to work for him. Gloom called him his 'old assistant' when he attacked us."

"What the lad said is a fact." Roger addressed the

others. "Gloom's story didn't get out. The Investigative Branch killed it in the press."

Pete absentmindedly twirled one of his ghostly curls. "How about getting us to Nevermore?"

"The safest way to enter," said Roger, "is through the Gate of Darkness."

Jiminy! Billy grimaced. *Don't like the sound of that!*

"That will take us directly to Diabolis, the Dark Side's capital city. As for Nevermore, that's where family connections come into play again," Roger explained. "It seems, every so often, Shadewick Gloom separates some new soul from the pack for a personal welcome."

"I can vouch for that," Ned offered. "Seen 'em cut from the herd myself. After we've turned them over to the Receiving Department, of course. Haven't lost a soul on *my* watch yet." He tapped his chest bones proudly.

Roger continued, "So it's a matter of getting up into Government Hall. Then we tag along with Ned to the Receiving Department, and *finally* bluff our way to Gloom's office. After that, you're on your own. I plan to wish myself back."

Doesn't sound like much of a plan. "What happens when we get there?" Billy looked at Pete with alarm.

"That's where we'll employ a little pirate stealth,"

101

Pete said casually. "Don't ye think I learned a trick or two in all me years at sea?"

But at this, even Jenkins squawked skeptically.

Ned dipped a look toward Roger. "I'll get you to the Receiving Department and that's it . . . even if it means less gold in my pocket."

"Well I'm going every bit of the way," Billy insisted. His resolve felt pieced together by plasters and splints, but he promised himself he wouldn't let Millicent down no matter how his knees wanted to wobble.

As the group prepared to leave, Minnie Lumbus wished her son a stiff (even by skeleton standards) goodbye, then turned to Billy. "You take care of Pete, you hear?" She sniffed and wiped a foggy tear with her sleeve. "And take care of yourself, too. There's a mighty big chance I'll never see you again if you make the smallest slipup." She patted Billy's bottom, pushing him on his way. "So don't!"

On his way out, Pete reached up for a package on top of the coat rack. It was wrapped in brown paper and string, but Billy was sure it contained something special. *Some kind of magical talisman to ward off evil? Or a cloak to make us invisible?*

"Ye'll just have to wait and see," said Pete, his glass eye glimmering.

Chapter 15
Dreads

Shadewick Gloom snatched Millicent's hair and glided her farther into the depths of Nevermore. It was a discombobulating sensation, even for someone not altogether there. Along with the tombs and tippy mausoleums, some plots were filled with freshly dug graves. Scattered here and there were a number of smaller structures housing underground burial chambers. Shadewick's smile was especially fond whenever they passed these crypts.

Not everyone was trapped inside. Several blocks away, a small group of groundskeepers were pruning hedges, digging holes, and raking dead leaves. Sniffing the air, they turned slowly as Millicent and Gloom passed.

A battered skeleton was digging a grave. He was only a head taller than Millicent. At first she thought he was a skeleton boy, but on a second examination, he moved like an older man. The skeleton paused as they approached. A gelatinous gob encased his head, held on by a squishy mass of tendrils.

"What's that?" Millicent gasped.

As architect of Nevermore, Gloom took delight in explaining such things. He dangled Millicent over the lip of the grave and held forth. "That, my dumpling, is a dread."

"It's disgusting!"

"How kind!" Pleasure shimmered through Shadewick's smile as he gestured toward the skeleton's head. "See how the creature's sack envelops the victim and the tendrils reach inside to penetrate the brain? Saddled up there on the head, the dread plants fear like seeds, then reaps the resulting nightmares and screams. Being trapped by a dread is the worst way of all to spend your eternity here in Nevermore."

"But, why do you need dreads? This place seems bad enough," Millicent asked, literally breathless.

"Why? What a ridiculous question, my dear . . . you might as well suggest prisons abandon their guards, or the dungeons dispense with their thumbscrews. Outrageous!"

He chuckled as he leaned over the grave, inspecting the skeleton's work, and continued, "Along with keeping us well stocked in nightmares, they're very useful for keeping order around here. They can shatter the wills of my most resistant guests."

Inside its gelatinous casing, the dread unwrapped its tendrils from the skeleton's head, then probed them hungrily toward Millicent and the shadow hounds.

Shadewick jerked Millicent back from the grave's edge. "Such greedy things. Once they've defiled a victim, they're instantly hungry for something fresh . . . wouldn't want one latching on to you . . . leastwise, not yet," he snickered, dragging her to the carriage road.

Millicent looked back at the grave, with more white in her eyes than a hen's egg.

"For now, you'll take up residence in the snug little

crypt right over there. And Tongs will be nice enough to keep you company, won't you, boy? Yes, you will. Such a good, little, snarly, ripping, vicious doggy you are, tooooooo."

Tongs wagged his tail, prancing with excitement, but when he turned to Millicent, he was all business — big spiky teeth business. And that's how he continued to regard her as he and she were installed into the crypt. From the outside it looked like a small classical temple. Inside, a large stone staircase limited floor space. It led to the dank vault below.

Despite Tongs's watchful eye, Millicent managed to get close enough to the barred windows to see Gloom stop to admire the statuary lining the roof and other ornate touches, then sweep off toward the shadowport with Hammer frisking at his side.

Millicent drifted, rubbing her forehead and thinking, *All in all, this is NOT a very nice place.*

Chapter 16
By the Bell of St. Dunstable

Through Houndstooth-on-Codswattle they came, scores of skeletons, clattering into the graveyard next to St. Dunstable's. In its long history, the blocky Norman church had never seen such an unusual flock.

Mr. Bones surveyed the crowd with growing annoyance. What had him nettled was not the skeletons, most of whom had shown up on time. It was the church bell. Vicar Parsons had been ringing it when time stopped, locking the bell in a long *CLONNNNNNNNGGGG* ever since. The old codger stood frozen in the tower, oblivious to hundreds of skeletons rattling by.

At least Mr. Bones could count his blessings about the rain. The drops were still stuck in place.

Mr. Bones nodded to the Bunyons, residents of a local farmhouse, as they and their sons elbowed to the front of the crowd. The Headleys were also there, from the manor next door.

A few feet away, Mrs. Bones chatted with Mrs. Wormwood, the skeleton in charge of the town mortuary. Mrs. Wormwood was deaf as a deadbolt, so Mrs. Bones was forced to yell into her ear horn. Mrs. Bones excused herself with a genteel shout and took her place beside Mr. Bones.

The churchyard was well past capacity by now. Many skeletons were forced to clamber up on the crumbling walls or balance on tipping headstones. Mr. Bones consulted his pocket watch. Being set to Afterlife time, it was ticking merrily along.

"Right!" he clicked the lid shut and addressed the crowd. "Ladies, gentlemen! Your attention, *please!*"

But the crowd was still in a talkative mood.

He began again, "There *is* an F.A.D. emergency." Skeleton jaws stopped clacking. "And this is of particular importance to me because my brother, Grim, is the missing field agent."

Nearby, an old voice creaked, "Grim Bones has been kissing? What kind of emergency is that?" Mrs. Wormwood strained to hear more through her ear horn.

Mr. Bones ignored her. "I would like you to separate into groups of four, and work out to the edge of our jurisdiction. Be on the lookout for Grim's blue glow. It's a stroke of luck we have such a dreary day. It should make spotting him easier.

"Whatever overpowered Grim must be extraordinarily dangerous, so any skeletons under twelve years old should stay here. We'll use you as runners to gather reinforcements in case there's a need." Mr. Bones scanned the crowd. A sea of ivory faces looked back at him — some determined, some drained by fear. "Any questions?"

Mrs. Bones cast him a gentle smile as the jawing started up and a bony hand shot up in the crowd.

"Excuse me, Mr. Bones?" The hand belonged to Mrs. Ribtuck. Her knobbly features were reminiscent of a potato.

Mr. Bones, consulting a map, looked up. "Eh?"

Mrs. Ribtuck said, "My neighbor's not here."

"Who is it?"

Her reply —"Liam Slackbones"— left everyone shaking their heads.

Mr. Bones looked in the direction of Stonehamm Cottage, home of Mordecai Cleansington, and sighed. "Well, I guess that's no surprise. Probably sleeping on the job." Liam Slackbones's lazy reputation was well known. "I'm sorry, everyone. Looks like we should carry on."

But before the skeletons could turn again, Mrs. Bones said something that later caused Mr. Bones to thank his blessings he'd had the good sense to marry her, though at first he was quite annoyed.

"Lars," she whispered, "don't you think we should have a look anyway? You never know."

"I'll look a fool for changing my mind," he whispered back.

"Lars . . ." Her voice was beyond a whisper now. "How foolish will you look if something *did* happen and we're too late to help?"

Mr. Bones sighed and said, "Er . . . sorry, everyone. It's best we check."

Mr. Bunyon seemed amused by what looked to be a good spat brewing. He grinned like a picket fence. Mrs. Bunyon frowned at him. "I wouldn't smirk. You've been far more mulish."

With Mr. Bunyon properly shushed, the secrets-closet skeletons set off, each wondering what kind of power could overwhelm the most formidable skeleton in the Afterlife.

Chapter 17
Gateway to Darkness

A few blocks from the Boneyard, Ned assumed his official Skeleton Guide duties by collecting his transferees. They were twenty of the scruffiest ghosts Billy had ever laid eyes on. Billy was not happy to see Martha's Uncle Mordecai among them, but had to admit that he was not particularly surprised. Condemned prisoners in hand, the group marched out of Edgeton and crossed a quarter mile of barren plain. Ned drove the shackled ghosts double-time, so there was plenty of grumbling.

Like: "What's the rush? Dark Side running low on souls?" and, "I just died — you'd think a fellow could have a few minutes' peace."

When they arrived at the checkpoint, the sight greeting them quickly silenced their complaints.

A huge wall marked the Dark Side. It was a thousand

feet high and bristling with spikes. Nestled at its base lay a bustling skeleton cavalry encampment.

"How come bad guys don't go directly to the Dark Side when they die?" Billy asked. "You'd think that would be a lot simpler than collecting them all on this side and then sending them over there." Billy turned to Pete, who was fiddling with his package, so Roger answered. "The beings in the Realms Above trust us Lightsiders to do a better job of administrating judgment procedures. It's something like applying to university." He closed his eyes. "Let's see if I can remember all the steps.

"I arrived through the Tunnel of Light. After docking at the Hall of Reception, I was conducted to an immense lecture room, where a lengthy application form was waiting. That had to be filled out — then there's the biographical essay, of course. These were then packed off to the Realms Above. Sadly, no amount of family pull can help you there." Roger looked back toward the Edgeton sky. "Then, I had to wait." He gripped Billy's sleeve, turning his white knuckles whiter. "It felt like an eternity."

"Clackers! Were you nervous?" Billy was curious.

"I should guess I was! Felt like I was about to die all over again. But at last I had letter in hand, and when I finally worked up the nerve to open it up, it sparkled with a golden light. I was in!" Roger clacked his jaw into a bony grin.

The skeleton's smile was contagious, but melted from Billy's face when he turned toward the looming wall. Of all its spiky darkness, it was the gate that surprised him the most. Only the width of a single man, it shot up the towering wall in a ragged slash.

"Why's the door so narrow?" he asked Roger.

"I keep forgetting you're not from around here." Roger tipped back his top hat. "The gate into the Light Side is much the same. It has to do with responsibility."

"Responsibility?"

"Well, it's a narrow path with high-reaching consequences, good or bad. There's only enough room for one person to pass through, no matter how much we would like to blame others for our choices."

Billy squinted into the shadows atop the wall, feeling as if bats were flying through his missing belly.

A loud wail spilled over the wall. Billy turned to see Uncle Mordecai cringe. He was standing at the front of the line, about twenty yards away, and so wrapped in his worries he didn't notice the latest irregularity. But Billy did and couldn't help giggling.

The mystery of what had been in Pete's parcel was bouncing with a bustle right in front of him. The old pirate had slipped behind the guardhouse and was now sporting a lavender dress.

Pete muttered, "The things a fella's got to do to put things right," as he pulled a veiled hat over his head. It covered his features in what Roger insisted was a most becoming way.

The disguise didn't do much to cover Pete's ship-deck stride, and Billy thought his parrot, Jenkins, was a dead giveaway, too. So did Ned.

Pete gathered Billy close to his skirts. "Grim made up some documents for me. Has me travelin' as a skeleton. I'll tell the guards yer me grandson and that should get us through. There's a note attached says I'm to join up with a tour group at the Hornsley Hotel." He smiled at Billy from under his veil.

"A tour group?" Billy wondered. "Is there really such a thing?"

"Sure as a parrot's got pinfeathers." Pete nodded. Jenkins presented his wing in a sweeping bow.

"Some Lightsiders visit all the time"— Roger slipped into the conversation —"to remind themselves of how good they have it, but others like to strut around and lord it over the unfortunates."

Clops and jingles announced the approach of an officer mounted on a skeleton horse. He adjusted his monocle when he saw the group, but his gaze lingered on Pete. Tipping his helmet, he cooed, "We don't get many ladies traveling out here. It pleases me to see such an elegant flower."

Pete fluttered a whalebone fan, tittering in a squeaky voice. "Thank ye young man, yer a darlin'."

"He really has been out here a long time if *that's* his idea of a looker," Roger whispered to Billy.

Pete elbowed Roger in the ribs. Billy bit down hard, trying not to laugh.

"Not at all, madam . . . charmed." The officer bowed, his monocle dropping out of his eye socket. "My name is Colonel Siegely, commander of the Afterlife's third regiment of the Light Cavalry. Not sure if you've been apprised of the situation, but seems an Afterlife emergency's been declared — some kind of Hall of Reception foul-up."

"Try to act surprised," Pete whispered.

Billy did his best.

"'An extra-high level of security will be in effect, starting today,'" Colonel Siegely read from an official document he'd retrieved from a tunic pocket. "'We will be screening travelers for dangerous items such as shampoo and toothpaste. And you will also have to remove your shoes.'"

Pete fluttered his fan at the colonel. "Might we have a few words in private on that very point?" He twittered.

The colonel trotted his horse over at once, his bony face plastered with delight. "Certainly, madam." Siegely grunted as he dismounted.

"It's *mademoiselle* to ye. I'm unattached at present." Pete tapped him with the tip of the folded fan. "Perhaps you could do a kindness to a lady and her grandson."

"Grandson, it can't possibly be! I was certain that you were going to say brother."

"Again, ye have me blushin'. But ye see, we have a

little dilemma." Pete stationed Billy between the advancing officer and himself. "Perhaps ye'll be good enough to help us."

"Your servant, mademoiselle!" The colonel responded with a bow.

"We need to sneak a few golden wishes in, so we can wish our way out if we don't like the accommodations. I'm a touch finicky, ye see."

"Understandable, but normally out of the question. If a Darksider ended up with a golden wish, he could wish himself over to the Light Side, too." The colonel adjusted his monocle, his eyes focusing for the first time. "I do get that request every so often, but not from skeletons. Never seen one rich enough to manage it."

"Err . . ." Pete hemmed.

The colonel frowned. Billy had to think of something quick. And as luck would have it, he didn't have to stray very far from the truth. "Candy!" he blurted.

"Ehhh?" Both Colonel Siegely and Pete turned to Billy.

"Candy," Billy repeated. "We've made our fortune in candy. We're very well-to-do."

"How delightful!" Colonel Siegely hitched in his paunchy jacket and puffed out his chest. "Even I like a tidbit now and again. Perhaps I can overlook the golden wishes for today." He looked at Pete longingly and took another step forward.

Not good. Billy winced. *Come on. Think of something!*

The colonel's horse snorted.

"What's your horse's name?" Billy asked frantically.

Colonel Siegely looked down at Billy. "What's that, young man?"

"Your horse . . . he's a real bruiser. What's his name?"

The colonel locked an admiring glance on the animal. "His name is Clattershanks, and I say he's the finest in the Afterlife."

Clattershanks lifted his head and whinnied proudly. But Billy was pretty sure Fleggs could vaporize this horse with one hoof.

Billy asked all about the horse: how many times he'd seen action, what was his favorite saddle, and how fast he could gallop.

The colonel answered. And about twenty minutes later, he gave a cursory look at their documents. Before Colonel Siegely clacked back to the guardhouse, he left Billy and Pete with a warning. "Keep your coins well hidden. If someone were to find out I let them pass, well, they'd be leading me in there next — and all for a pretty girl." He tipped his helmet to Pete. "I'll count the days until your safe return."

Pete curtsied, then he and Billy and all the shackled ghosts headed toward darkness. Seconds later a horn blew notes so deep they could have been ripped from a thunderstorm's belly. The gate ratcheted open, and a blast of heat nearly boiled the marrow in Billy's bones.

Chapter 18
The High Council

As Billy and Pete were sorting out the state of emergency, members of the High Council were planning actions of their own. Their chamber floated in a place of honor, well above Celesdon. It was the shape of a glowing orb, covered in a network of silver supports and crystal windows. For many years it had been the Afterlife's symbol of truth, but lately its sheen had dulled.

Inside the vast dome, council members' desks were set in a ring, and a circular opening in the middle gave a spectacular view of the skyline below. Marble benches rimmed the room. This gallery was usually packed with civic-minded citizens, but now the seats stood silent.

Miss Chippendale and her supporters favored one side of the chamber. Oversecretary Underhill and a wrinkled old wraith — the only other honest soul left on the council — sat on the opposite side. The wraith stared at Miss Chippendale with unwavering disdain.

Behind the council members, their assistants busily scribbled notes and passed them to waiting cherub pages. The pages buzzed through the dome, dispensing and retrieving council messages. Air traffic was especially thick on Miss Chippendale's side of the room.

"All rise," said the Sergeant at Arms.

Everyone stood as a blindfolded woman in sheer white robes materialized in a throne. This was Justice. Her hair and robes wafted about her as if stirred in a cup of ghostly tea. She hung her scales on the side of the throne and nodded almost imperceptibly to the Sergeant at Arms. "Be seated," he intoned.

"First order of business." Miss Chippendale jumped to her feet.

"The council member from the Investigative Branch is recognized." The Sergeant solemnly banged his staff.

"I move the chambers be sealed for a members-only secret session," Miss Chippendale proclaimed.

Oversecretary Underhill instantly clacked up on his bony feet. "I move that the chamber remain open! How can Justice be served behind closed doors?" Council members looked away; some even snickered up their sleeves. "How?" His shouts echoed around the chamber.

In a voice neutral as a line down the middle, Justice answered the skeleton. "I cannot pretend that I am happy by the direction that some in this chamber have taken lately"— the manifestation turned to Miss Chippendale's side of the room —"but these decisions are arrived at through a vote of the majority. Lord Underhill, while I laud your intentions, I am powerless to oblige you."

Justice sat back and the proceedings continued. The chamber was emptied of all assistants and pages; then the crystal dome dimmed — obscuring any view of Celesdon.

When the Sergeant at Arms pounded the council back to order, Miss Chippendale stood for her next bit of business. "Today we are faced with an almost inconceivable danger! Earthly time has made an unscheduled stop, threatening the very foundation of the Afterlife itself. We've been caught unprepared. Small power outages are already dotting Celesdon." A murmur echoed through the chamber. "Eternal energy, the source of all Afterlife magic, has been cut off by *this* traitor"— Miss Chippendale scowled at Underhill —"and his chief field agent, Grim!"

"LIES!" Underhill slapped his bony hands on his desk.

"Isn't it true that time has stopped on Earth?" Miss Chippendale smirked.

"Yes, but —"

"Isn't Grim Bones the only one with the proper credentials to stop time," Miss Chippendale thundered on, "and isn't the length of this time stoppage unauthorized?"

"Yes, but —"

"Isn't he under your direct command? And didn't he, under your command, contact Glass-Eyed Pete, a known anti-Afterlife operative?"

Lord Underhill stood in stunned silence.

"I have proof. Several letters with Grim Bones's private address were found by my agents at Endmoor Castle." Miss Chippendale held up the parchments in a victorious fist.

"Where is your warrant? You broke into his castle without one!"

"There's a state of emergency. I don't need one! We must issue a subpoena immediately!" Miss Chippendale urged her side of the council. "If Grim Bones doesn't appear before this council within the half hour next, we should brand him an outlaw along with his ill-bred master — Oversecretary Underhill!"

Chapter 19
Millicent's Crypt

For the longest time the skeleton gravedigger kept to his business and paid Millicent no mind. Inside the crypt, Tongs stood, paws up, on the window ledge, staring through the bars. Every so often, a drop of his shadowy drool plinked on the stone floor.

Millicent wished the big lug would get out of the way. He was blocking her view. She shoved her hands into her dress pockets as she drifted around the crypt's small perimeter — thankful at least that in her semi-solid state Gloom hadn't been able to lock her in the vault below.

Something rustled outside the door. Millicent called out, "Who's there?" not altogether sure she really wanted to know.

The tip of a pickaxe smashed through, sending splinters dancing across the floor. The next strike shattered the lock and the door creaked open. Standing outside was the gravedigger. The dread atop his head burbled and sparked. Its tentacles stretched greedily toward Millicent and Tongs.

The skeleton dropped his pick and lurched forward. Tongs licked his chops and sprang, latching on to an arm bone. Burbling something that sounded like "yum!" the dread shot a mass of tendrils out, lassoing the dog. By the time Tongs hit the floor, the dread had pulled its gelatinous body over his head and was ravenously feasting.

The skeleton tottered a few steps. His eyes slowly creaked open. "L-l-lucky dog is a delicacy in these parts."

He offered Millicent a thin smile, then leaned heavily against the door, examining his hands as if they'd been lost in the post and had just turned up on his doorstep. "Gosh it's good to be free of that thing and under my own steam again!"

Millicent bent down for the pickaxe; she could only lift it a few inches before her fingers slipped through the handle. "Bother!" she grumped. "Grab that pick and let's go!"

The skeleton groaned as he staggered over to the pick and dragged it out of the crypt. Millicent drifted behind him, wishing every second she could run.

"Can you jam the door, to trap the dog?" she asked.

The skeleton looked around. "With what? The pick?"

"No, we'll need that to free the others."

An ornamental statue stared down at Millicent from atop the crypt. It looked as if it wanted to escape the place as much as Millicent. *Sorry, she* thought sadly, *but you're needed here.* "How about that statue? Can you tumble it down?"

"Looks doable." The skeleton gauged the angle of the roof, but after clattering topsides, he called down, "Got a bit of trouble heading our way!"

Millicent spun around. Sure enough a group of

dread-headed groundskeepers was a block away and stumbling closer.

"Not much time for introductions," he said, scuttling up to the roof's peak. "But what's your name? Mine's Bartemis Brittleback."

The name sounded familiar to Millicent. She struggled to place it. "Mine's Millicent Hues."

"Pleasure, Millicent. Say, I think I read about you in the *Eternal Bugle* last year." He windmilled his arms, fighting to rebalance. "Something to do with Commissioner Pickerel. Grim Bones was involved . . . and a boy. Weren't they?"

Millicent was surprised by her notoriety in the Afterlife, and then remembered where she'd heard his name. "You've been in the paper, too. You're in charge of the Skeleton Guild."

"Guilty as charged." He chuckled as he latched on to the statue. "Although not altogether sure why I've been sentenced to *this* place."

"My mom and dad are here, too," Millicent sighed. "We need to save them."

"So long as we save ourselves somewhere along the way."

Mr. Brittleback put his shoulder to work, rocking the statue on its base. It crashed to the ground. He scampered off the roof and then, with an effort that nearly popped off his shoulder blades, propped the statue against the door.

Mr. Brittleback glanced at the closing groundskeepers. "I suggest we find someplace to hide, then sneak back when it's safer to see about your parents."

"I'm not so sure."

"Being sure would be a terribly good thing right about now." He stopped and looked back. "They're just about in our laps."

"You're pretty handy with a shovel." Millicent gestured to the grave. "I think we should make a stand."

"We?" Mr. Brittleback looked at her wispy form. "You mean *me*."

"I would love to have a whack at those things" — Millicent stamped a ghostly foot — "but you'll just have to do with me cheering you on."

"You are a bossy little bee, aren't you?" Brittleback grinned as he clattered over to the grave. "Dreads," he said, limbering up with a few swings of the long-handled shovel, "prepare for the realms down under."

Chapter 20
Diabolis

The Gate of Darkness closed behind Billy. The squeal of its hinges sounded like cutting laughter, as if finding humor in his mission.

"Well done, me boy. Ye got us out of a real scrape." Pete tossed his disguise behind a nearby boulder.

"Perhaps you shouldn't have shown quite so much ankle." Roger chuckled.

"I got me sword now. It would be a shame if all yer fine hair got a sudden trimmin'," Pete cautioned.

Roger's chuckle bloomed into a hearty laugh.

Billy didn't hear any of this. He was too busy with the view before them. Diabolis.

The capital city of the Dark Side — the place was horrifying and yet mesmerizing at the same time. It stood on the other side of a mile-wide pit. A narrow bridge, whose arcing supports were lost to darkness, stretched to the main gate.

Behind city rooftops, the air was ablaze with flames, pouring into the sky as though they were illuminated curtains. The buildings were made of marble columns and low-pitched roofs, but there wasn't a straight line to be found anywhere. Every angle was more wicked than the next.

Billy kept his eyes focused ahead as they made their way across the bridge. Whenever he peeked over the rails it felt as if the depths were wrapping around his wobbling knees and pulling him toward the edge.

From halfway across the bridge, the residents looked like insects, scurrying in and out of temples, shops, and hovels. Billy was pretty sure a number of them *were* insects, but much larger than the garden-variety bug.

Diabolis proper (if one really can use that word) was a tumult of demons and lost souls. In general everyone paid little attention to anyone else — at least until they were hungry.

Ned marched the conscripts through a narrow street. Temples dedicated to each of the seven deadly sins lined each side. Activity was particularly fierce around the temples dedicated to Wrath and Pride. All was quiet at the temple of Sloth. And the flabby souls at the temple of Gluttony looked tantalized when Billy and company marched by.

Billy realized they wouldn't have made it past the city's threshold if it hadn't been for Ned. The skeleton and his very busy staff had cut a path through every crowd.

"Where are we headed?" Billy asked Pete as Ned's staff sent another demon arcing over the crowd.

The old pirate glanced at Government Hall overhead. At the point where it arched above the Dark Side wall, its unswerving architecture had changed into snaking shadowy curves. "The Receiving Department's up that way. But first, we got to pass through that thing over there."

Billy traced Pete's eye line from Government Hall to the place where it intersected the top of a mountainous building shaped like a demon head. It towered over the shopping district, about a quarter of a mile away. But the size of the thing made it feel much closer. The building's stone eyes seemed particularly attentive, and Billy thought he saw the mouth grow a little wider.

A tentacled demon with wiggly eyestalks tripped Billy. "Watch your step!" it burbled. "Maybe I should teach you some manners!"

It changed its mind, however, when it saw Ned's staff, and hastily skedaddled into a nearby deli. There were other eating establishments at hand, crawling with customers and even crawlier food. Inside, patrons enjoyed their victims with fine wine rather than grabbing a quick bite out on the street.

Marshmallow shops were especially trendy here, as were roasting-stick shops. There were tourist traps, too. Billy was appalled to see some Lightsiders caught like flies on a huge sticky web.

But it was a ghost family — a mother, father, and daughter — that drew Billy's attention with their stares. Like the squirming tourists, it was clear they were from the Light Side. The father glanced at his copy of the *Eternal Bugle* and then at Pete. Before Billy could warn anyone, the father shouted, "I recognize you. You're a traitor!" He corralled his wife and daughter and pulled them away. "I'm getting the authorities!"

The daughter stammered, "C-come off it, Dad. Leave them alone!"

In another situation and at another time, Billy thought he would have liked this girl. She was as spunky as Millicent in the way she stood up to her dad. But the thought of Millicent only made him worry more. Was he already too late to save her? Was Uncle Grim done for, too? As Billy tussled with these dark thoughts, the family disappeared in a shimmer of gold light. *Looks like we aren't the only ones sneaking wishes.*

Angry shouts ripped toward them from a half block away. Billy looked up. "Uhm . . . I think we should go." He retreated, his boot clinking ever so slightly.

Two sentinels were moving toward them, parting the crowd like seagoing steamers.

"You better hope they pass," Ned hissed, "or you're on your own!"

"Shouldn't we run?" Billy squeaked.

"Hold fast!" Pete ordered. "That'll just get their attention."

"And the crowd's, too," Roger added.

Pete traded nervous looks with Roger but didn't let

Billy see him. Uncle Mordecai and the rest of the conscripts huddled together, pulling as far away as their chains would allow. Even Ned bit a bony knuckle.

"Criminy! *Look* at those two!" If Billy had been wearing his body instead of bones, his heart would have been thumping like a timpani drum.

The sentinels arrived, riding on two gigantic spiders. The first demon must have stood a story tall, the second, a half a story taller. Each sentinel was covered in ruby-colored scales transparent enough to show pulsing organs beneath. Their domed helmets could have been from ancient Greece, and the leathery wings hanging from their backs could have made fine mainsails on the *Spurious II*. Billy tried to disappear into Pete's coattails.

The crowd jostled elbows as it pressed back. One spindly demon wearing a smoking jacket lost his cigar in the confusion. It bounced off paving stones and rolled to Pete's boot. Billy untangled himself from coattails and looked down. And that's when his good nature got the best of him. He picked up the cigar and handed it back. The demon snatched it, a look of confusion blinking in its button-sized eyes.

"No man shall a good deed do," rumbled the first sentinel in a voice so low it could have bubbled up from the earth's bunions.

"Nor woman, child, or demon, nor any creature fair or foul," the second sentinel added. They spoke mechanically, as if every thing they said was by rote. "It is the first and only rule."

"Well I should say that covers just about everyone." Roger eyed the guards with defiance. "Except for us. We're Lightsiders."

Rules? Here? Billy scratched his head. His ivory finger sounded as if it were writing questions on a blackboard.

They thumped down from their saddles, each holding a long spear with a crescent blade. "Silence, skeleton!" The smaller sentinel swung his spear blade an inch from Roger's nose holes.

"Hey, wait a minute!"

Billy looked around, wondering who had said such an ill-advised thing. Then he realized the words had leaped out of his own mouth. Splitting the air in a whoosh, the sentinels' spears now pointed an inch from *his* nose holes.

"Here's the un-troublemaker." The lead sentinel nodded to the bigger one. "Do we take him to the inquisitor for questioning? Or eat him here?"

Billy stepped back nervously. His boot clinked. Such a tiny sound, but it was loud enough to send Billy's fortune in the decidedly wrong direction. Starting with upside down. The bigger sentinel raised Billy high over-head and shook him like a piggy bank.

Clinkety-tink. Billy's golden coin danced on the cob-blestones. His hope for escape spun on its rim and rolled away. The crowd surged forward. Uncle Mordecai's eyes sparked green as he yanked the chained ghosts into the fray. But the smaller sentinel swept up the coin before anyone could get to it.

The larger sentinel dropped Billy bottom-first and scooped up Pete and Roger. A few shakes later the sen-tinels had retrieved every coin. Billy scrambled to his feet, furious at himself for not doing a better job of hiding his wish. But there was nothing to be done about it — no going back now.

The smaller sentinel clinked the coins in his palm as if trying to decide what to do with them, and then he rumbled, "We must take these Lightsiders below for interrogation."

"Sorry to be so disagreeable," Roger piped in, "but that would be highly inadvisable."

Billy thought Roger seemed awfully cool about it, seeing as they were about to be introduced to the inner workings of a blast furnace.

"Inadvisable?" the smaller sentinel asked. "And why would that be, skeleton?"

"Because"— Roger stifled a yawn —"we've been asked to bring this fine new soul to Shadewick Gloom." He gestured to Martha's uncle.

"Whaa?" Uncle Mordecai's mouth dropped open.

Both sentinel helmets turned robotically toward the old man.

"Ye best get him to Gloom's office straightaway. He'd be mighty sad to hear that ye delayed us." Pete snuck a smile toward Billy.

The smaller sentinel's empty helmet scanned Pete up and down and then turned to his partner. "I will take the conscript to Gloom. You take the good-deed doer to the inquisitor."

Billy screwed up his eyes, straining to think what to do. And once more, the truth served him. "Oh, he'll want to see me . . . and my friends!" he said, sweeping a hand toward Pete and Roger: but missed Ned, who was doing his best to blend in with the conscripts.

"Huh?" Roger straightened up.

Pete was quicker to recover. "The lad's not pullin' yer tails, neither." He frowned at the sentinels. "Has a standing invitation by Gloom's office whenever he's in the Dark Side."

"I'm sure he'd be furious if you didn't let me see him," Billy said with loads more confidence than he felt.

Chapter 21
At Gloom's Door

"Where is everyone?" Billy asked Pete. "This place looks deserted."

Billy had always imagined that Government Hall would be filled with the churn of administrative activity. At least that's how his parents and Mr. Benders had always described it.

"Not a lot for these bureaucrats to do, I suspect." Pete looked around. "Ye heard the sentinels say there's only the one rule 'bout not doing good deeds."

Billy, Pete, and Roger stood near the door of the Receiving Department, trying to look as inconspicuous as possible. They had no wish to be invited inside. Thanks to the sentinels, they had no wishes at all. Uncle Mordecai stood a few paces away, still wearing shackles. His chains clinked gently each time he sneaked a nervous glance into the office.

Ned had insisted that the sentinels stop at the

Receiving Department, before he turned over Mordecai. He also had pointed out that it was his duty as a
Skeleton Guide to return to the Light Side once his prisoners had been discharged.

The trip up to Government Hall had been unevent-
ful, if you consider a clattering ride suspended over a pit
of flames an everyday activity. The sentinels had been
monstrously rough with the crowds as they escorted
Billy and company through the streets. But they had
been almost tender with their spider mounts as they
urged them up the walls of the elevator shafts and then
into the long hallway, where they were silently standing guard.

Looking up at the demons, Billy scratched his head. "They're awfully good at following orders."

"That's all a part of evil's bloom," Pete agreed. "It blossoms best when people blindly follow orders."

A *BANG, CLANK, CLANG* of steam pipes drew Billy's attention to the Receiving Department door.

ABANDON HOPE, ALL YE WHO ENTER (THEN SURREN-DER THE REST OF YOUR PERSONAL EFFECTS) was chiseled into the stonework above the entrance. Roger told Billy that the last living person to visit the Dark Side had come up with the first part of the line — some Italian fellow, Dante. The demons had just loved the quote.

Inside the office, a chubby demon wearing a singed waistcoat and a very bored expression stamped the ghosts' paperwork. Every time the stamp rapped paper, the documents burst into flames and the ghosts standing before him transformed into the most gruesome shapes. Some grew horns and tiny bat wings (like the chubby demon), some tentacles or tails, and others multiple eyestalks with big dripping fangs. Back in the hallway Uncle Mordecai paled and turned away from the door.

Pete sidled closer to Roger. "Looks like yer with us for the long haul."

Stroking his hair, the skeleton dandy looked down

the long curved hallway, then up at the towering sentinels. His lidded eyes seemed like calculators figuring
the odds of escape. Roger slouched back against the
wall. "It's just the opportunity to develop an interest in
Dark Side architecture."

"Sorry. Telling them Gloom wanted to see me was
the only thing I could think of," Billy apologized.

"Just as well you did, Billy, otherwise I'd be a top hat
taller from the inquisitor's rack," Roger said. "Besides, I
did promise you I'd get you to Gloom's door."

Just then, Ned emerged, humming and holding a
transfer receipt. He tucked it temporarily under his arm
and then set about his final official duty. He unlocked
Uncle Mordecai's cuffs, setting him free. "Well, that's
that. It's back to Edgeton for me." He tapped his staff to
his forehead in a salute, then caught the look of Billy's
disappointment. "Nope, my mind's made up, Billy. Skeleton horses couldn't get me to change it."

"I'm sure yer mum will be plumb proud ye made it
this far," Pete said as Jenkins tut-tutted from the old pirate's shoulder.

Ned looked from Pete to Roger to Billy's misting
eyes, then rolled up his document and stuffed it into his
red cloak. "I'm sorry, Billy. I really am, but I can't risk it.
Got to go."

Ned pushed Mordecai over to Roger. Embarrassment shrouded the Skeleton Guide's expression as he slumped into the elevator. The metal floor grate groaned, and fingers of orange light lit him from below like prison bars shutting across his face.

Giving Billy a mournful wave, Ned called, "Good luck, boy."

With a deep metallic *THUNK* the elevator shrugged into use. Chain links the size of rib cages rattled through subterranean gears. Squeaks of protesting metal echoed through the long hallway with the disorder of scattering roaches.

The level of Billy's worry rose with each clattering link as Ned lowered out of sight. They never would have gotten this far without the skeleton's stout staff and alert scouting. And now Ned was leaving right when he and Gramps Pete were facing the most dangerous part of their journey.

Pete glanced over the edge of the elevator shaft. Scowl dwindling, he turned to Billy and Roger. "It won't do to fanny around. We best be going," he said. "This ain't a place for cowards." Then, striding up the hall, he beckoned everyone to follow.

Billy scampered up to join Pete and Roger, glad to be away from the sounds now emanating from the

Receiving Department. He refused to imagine what was happening to the conscripts now that they had been turned over. But the thought didn't seem to be eluding Uncle Mordecai. His eyes were round as golden wishes as he trudged along, looking back over his shoulder. The sentinels spurred their mounts forward. One took up the rear, keeping a missing eye on Billy. The other rode his spider to the head in order to lead the way.

"Any more ideas for a plan? Or is piratey stealth the best you've got?" Roger whispered to Pete.

"Stow it!" Pete growled. Then under his breath muttered, "Weren't sure we'd even get this far."

This did not improve Billy's confidence. Still, Pete and Roger sauntered along — Roger with a skimp of a smile on his face, like he hadn't a care in the world. Billy wondered where he found that kind of courage and if he might borrow a spoonful.

Soon the Receiving Department disappeared behind one hallway curve and then another. The longer they trudged, the more convoluted the hallway became. Billy could see firsthand why it wasn't wise to wish oneself around on the Dark Side.

Through roundabouts, dark distortions, and in and

out of backtracks the sentinel led them, until they arrived at a towering ebony door. Gloom's door. As it loomed above Billy, he couldn't shake the feeling it lead to the very depths of a nightmare — one that might last forever.

Chapter 22
The Skeleton Siege

When the skeletons arrived at Stonehamm Cottage, it was still thunderously dark. Mr. Bones gestured for everyone to gather around. Mrs. Bones, Mrs. Ribtuck, the two Headleys, and four Bunyons formed a tight huddle. Then Mr. Bones said, "Before we charge in there all willy-nilly, I suggest we do a little investigating. Mr. Headley, will you join me? The rest of you guard either side of the door. If something's in there, it might come this way." Mrs. Bones's brave look calmed him slightly as he turned to Headley. "Shall we?"

"We shall," Mr. Headley replied, and the two skeletons stole around the corner.

The bedroom window lit up with a sudden burst of purple as they drew near. Mr. Bones pressed his back against the cottage clapboards, then signaled silently for Headley to take up a post on the opposite side. Headley ducked under the sill and got into position. More glows erupted, followed by screams, and then the skeletons peeked inside.

The glass was filthy with dust, but what Mr. Bones saw was enough to chill him to the marrow. Millicent and a plump woman stood frozen next to a bed. *What is Millicent doing here? And where is Billy?*

Eyes flared with worry, Mr. Bones stepped in front of the window for a better look. The bed contained a wiry old man. In the center of the room, a shadowy shape slipped between two skeletons, suspended in the purple light of some unearthly magic. The skeletons were slumped forward, backs to the window.

Mr. Bones recognized Grim's cloak immediately. He guessed the other skeleton was Liam Slackbones. Mr. Bones scanned the room for Billy and Fleggs. *Maybe they've escaped.* But his flicker of hope vanished as the next purple flash revealed a third skeleton. Shadewick Gloom!

"We don't want any witnesses, now do we?" Gloom said — voice muffled by glass — as he applied a shimmering arc of purple energy to Liam Slackbones's skull. "That ought to boil that pea brain of yours!"

Mr. Bones grabbed the windowsill. It splintered apart in his hands.

"What's the matter?" Mr. Headley asked in a sharp whisper.

Mr. Bones's eyes were blank as a cemetery statue's. He slowly reached for the scar at his temple.

"It's no time to go wobbly." Mr. Headley grabbed Mr. Bones's shoulder and shook. "How are you going to save anyone like that?"

Very slowly, beneath twitching lids, the blue luminance returned to Mr. Bones's eyes. He steadied himself on the remains of the sill. "Right."

"Let's get in there."

"Not advisable," Mr. Bones groaned. "Not quite yet."

"We can't just stand here. That's plain wrong!"

"Of course it's wrong! But it's advisable."

Mr. Headley stared at Mr. Bones as if his head had turned into a parsnip.

"Don't think this doesn't pain me, Headley!"— Mr. Bones turned from the window in disgust —"but perhaps you haven't noticed his blasts are weakening: they always do." He closed his eyes, stroking his scar. "H-he doesn't have unlimited power."

"Apologies, Bones," Mr. Headley offered crisply. "That's why you're in charge."

"It shouldn't be long now. Let's get back to the others."

Mrs. Bones swept over to her husband as soon as he rounded the corner and she saw the extra paleness of his expression.

"I'm all right, my dear." Mr. Bones untangled himself from her embrace. He explained what was happening inside the cottage and finished with, "Let's give it a minute or so, then we will strike."

It was the longest minute Mr. Bones had ever withstood in his long Afterlife life. When the explosions from the room finally turned to fizzles, he signaled the others to follow.

The skeletons snuck craftily into the cottage and surrounded the bedroom door. On Mr. Bones's shout

of "You've tortured your last soul, Gloom!" they stormed in.

The skeletons clattered across the room — surrounding Gloom in a circle of Headleys, Bunyons, Boneses, and even a Ribtuck.

Mr. Bones stepped forward. "Nine to one, Gloom. Best to give up."

"Lars Bones!" The shadowy skeleton rasped his fingertips together, a jagged grin cutting across his jaw. "Whoever thought I'd see you again. Your nightmares were quite special. Such a shame I had to release you."

"We won't be releasing *you* anytime soon, I can tell you," Mr. Bones replied, hands trembling as he locked them tight behind his back.

Shadewick Gloom sauntered forward. Mr. Bones inched back nervously. "Nine to one you say? You think that's enough to hold back my kind of power? Ludicrous!"

"H-hold together," Mr. Bones urged the other skeletons. "He's bluffing. It will take him time to recharge."

"Look, Dad!" one of the Bunyon boys cried near the bed. "Grim Bones hasn't got his head!"

The skeletons turned to look. Indeed, Grim's hood was empty.

When they turned again to face Gloom, the odds had changed. It was now nine to two. Hammer bristled next to his master. The skeletons instinctively stepped back from the hound.

"Tear 'em up, boy!" Shadewick shouted. Shadowport key in hand, he fled to the nearest wall as the room burst into bone-clattering mayhem, with skeletons dashing in all directions.

But Mr. Bones threw himself at the nightmarish skeleton. "You're not going anywhere until you tell me what's happened to Billy!"

"Billy?" Gloom paused in midstride, then, like two blood-choked ticks, his eyes swelled with realization. "Of course. I should have remembered."

Turning his key with one hand, Gloom met Mr. Bones's charge with the other. The shadow skeleton had just enough power to deliver one more jolt. It seared Mr. Bones's temples, sending him to his knees, smoke drifting from his skull. Gloom sneered as he stepped through the shadowport and disappeared.

It was Mrs. Bunyon who finally restored order to the cottage. An enthusiastic thump to Hammer's head with her thighbone did the trick. The shadow hound was still laid out on the floor when Mr. Bones regained consciousness. Mrs. Bones helped her husband up and led him to Grim. Mr. Bones wobbled along, shaking his head as if trying to clear out cobwebs. The rest of the skeletons had congregated around Liam Slackbones, doing their best to bring him around.

Mr. Bunyon's barrel chest was near bursting with pride as he wrapped an arm around his wife, his sons on either side. "Saved the day, you did. Would 'a been a disaster without your quick wits and your thighbone."

"Weren't nothin' but a trifle." Mrs. Bunyon blushed.

"Well, it was just the trifle we needed." Mrs. Bones smiled, then turned to Mr. Bones. In the chaos, she hadn't heard Gloom mention Billy's name. "Do you think you can manage, Lars?" she asked as she let go of his arm.

Mr. Bones lurched over and swept open Grim's empty hood. "Billy's in real danger, I know it!"

"How?" Mrs. Bones asked, gripping Mr. Bones's shoulder.

"I saw it in Gloom's eyes."

Mr. Bones yanked Grim's body up by the lapels — his blue glow barely perceptible. "What's happened? Where's Billy?"

"Steady, Lars," Mrs. Bones soothed, although she was clearly as worried as he. "We need to think our way through this."

Screwing his eyes up, Mr. Bones lowered Grim back down. "Sorry, Brother."

"Fleggs is gone and so is Billy." Mrs. Bones rubbed her ivory brow, the way Millicent often did. "He must have escaped to the Afterlife."

"Most likely he's looking for Pete, but the old rascal has more hiding places than we have bones."

"Bones? Didn't Mr. Benders mention the Boneyard?"

"The Boneyard . . . yes, but it's anyone's guess where that is. And we've no way to get there."

Mrs. Bones's fingers flitted worriedly across her mouth, and then she stumbled to a chair and sat down. Mr. Bones reached after his wife, sad to see her brave front crumble.

"Someone say Boneyard? I could do with a little hair of the dog." Speaking thickly, Liam Slackbones sat up. "Gooo, I've a doozy. Feels like my head's split in two."

"You know the Boneyard?" Mr. Bones asked.

"Who doesn't? Drained many a glass there." He rubbed his head and looked around. "Where'd that shadowy gent go? A real troublemaker he was. Got in my way of getting back to the Department of Fibs and Fabrications."

Liam reached for his official D.F.F. pocket watch, mumbling, "Head's packed full of the worst kind of nightmares. Saint Bastian's Bones! I best get up there right now before it's too late!"

"Hang on a minute, Liam," Mr. Bones suggested. "Perhaps I can hitch a ride as long as you have a pass."

"Excellent idea, Bones!" Headley boomed, then grew thoughtful. "But how are you going to get around in the Afterlife without any golden wishes?"

Mr. Bones fingered his vest pockets. "I'm not sure, but being there has to be better than being here. Maybe I can get to Oversecretary Underhill's office. . . ."

"Maybe you should get to Fleggs instead," Mrs. Bones fretted. "It could be the fastest way to Billy."

"Good idea, but we're not sure where Fleggs is. And it will take more wishes than I have to find him."

"Whatever you're going to do, Mr. Bones, I wish you'd hurry." Liam glanced toward the bed and frowned. "With my charge gone, my pass is about to expire, and then I'll be stuck at Stonehamm Cottage for good."

Mr. Bones looked desperately from skeleton to

skeleton, searching for suggestions. One by one, they shrugged their shoulders, except for Mr. Bunyon. He was studying Grim. "Dunno, Mr. Bones, but isn't your brother rather well off in the Afterlife? . . . I should think he has a few golden wishes jingling his coin purse." He leaned down for a closer inspection.

Mr. Bones swept past Mr. Bunyon and rifled through Grim's pockets.

"Brilly-frilly-ill-iant, Mr. Bunyon!" Mr. Bones cried seconds later, holding up a palmful of golden wishes.

"Nicely done!" Mr. Headley pounded Mr. Bunyon on the back.

"No time to celebrate. We've got to crack on." Mr. Bones wrestled Grim's body up and wedged it under an arm. "Liam, grab hold." His legs buckled under the strain. Grim was terrifically heavy for a skeleton, particularly one without a head. Not surprising, though, with the responsibility for every soul on Earth weighing him down.

"Once we locate Fleggs, I may need your services at the Boneyard," Mr. Bones grunted.

"I've no problem with that." Liam rubbed his mouth with the back of a bony hand. When Grim's body was secure, Liam held up a piece of parchment. A thin line of silver light worked its way from the edges into its center. The D.F.F. document collapsed into flakey ashes as a purple glowing portal opened before them.

The last sight Mr. Bones saw of Stonehamm Cottage was the luminous eyes of his wife, pleading for him to be careful.

Chapter 23
Gloom and Doom

The sentinels bundled Billy, Pete, Roger, and Uncle Mordecai into Shadewick Gloom's vestibule, then took up guard positions on either side of the door. One of them had taken Pete's sword. It looked like a knitting needle in the demon's massive hand.

Opposite the prisoners stood a table holding Gloom's prize possessions. And tucked into alcoves, bookcases, and wall sconces were more. Altogether his bell jar collection numbered fifty heads: some from ghosts, others were skulls, and there were even a few ex-heads of state. But the center of the rambling table was reserved for the collection's crown jewel.

"Uncle Grim!" Billy cried, bounding forward, but a quick flick of a sentinel's spear pole sent him sprawling. If he hadn't been buttoned tight in his raincoat, his bones would have scattered everywhere.

"Hold fast, Billy," Pete whispered.

The disturbance woke several heads. Their muffled wails vibrated among the crystal domes, waking others. Grim blearily opened his eyes, his blue glow guttering like a nearly spent flame. "Hurry," he mouthed to Billy, and then his eyes flickered shut.

Billy couldn't tell if this was so he could concentrate, or if Grim had passed out. Sitting up, he shouted, "We will!" not having the faintest clue how he would go about hurrying anything along. Still, it was good to see his uncle again — even so tiny a portion of him.

Billy's relief lasted only as long as the time it takes to open a shadowport.

"Oooooh, presents for me? How thoughtful," Shadewick Gloom's warbling voice echoed as he strode up the hallway.

The sentinels snapped to attention. "They said you were expecting them, so we brought them here," one explained with a salute.

"And we found the prisoners with these." The larger sentinel held out the golden wishes.

Shadewick Gloom brushed past Billy and snatched the coins. "Naughty, naughty." He turned to the prisoners, flipping a coin off his ivory thumb. It spun in the air, held in place by Gloom's magical gaze. "Didn't anyone tell you you're not supposed to bring these over to the Dark Side?"

Tossing up the rest of the coins, the shadowy skeleton dispatched them with a squiggling purple arc of energy. Flecks of gold drifted slowly like wounded snowflakes and melted into the floor. Pete grabbed for his empty scabbard, Roger grimaced at the squandering of perfectly good gold, and Mordecai looked as if he wanted to melt away himself. But Billy was surprised by the weakness of the blast. Back at Stonehamm Farm, Shadewick Gloom's bolts had rocked the cottage.

"Seems I was wasting my time on Earth," Shadewick Gloom mused as he sidled toward his bell jar collection. With a sharp finger bone he plinked the crystal holding Grim. "A lucky stroke you were the perfect bait." Shadewick Gloom's gaze circled the room, then landed smack on Billy. "Not a totally useless trip, though. I did get reacquainted with your dad."

The look on Gloom's face would have made a shark blanch.

"Reacquainted?" Billy croaked. His heart felt as if it were trying to climb into his throat even though it wasn't there.

"Oh yes! Lars Bones, expert secrets keeper, master of fibs and fabrications. I didn't just tuck him away when he was last in Nevermore. No. He was one of my favorites. You should have seen him squirm when I introduced him to a few of my favorite interrogation techniques. Too bad the Investigative Branch was forced to release him. I did hate tossing him back."

"You . . . you're the one who gave him that scar," Billy gasped.

"Well, in a roundabout way, yes. But *you* are the one who really deserves the credit." Gloom glided toward Billy, his shadow robes wafting like smoke. "He squealed out the whole story. How you'd come to the closet . . . how he, your mother, and your uncle conspired to break so many of the Afterlife rules — especially when your uncle brought you back to life. I didn't put all that together until I saw your dad a few minutes ago."

Billy blinked as if he'd been stunned by a photographer's flash.

Gloom's eyes brightened when he saw remorse sweep across Billy's face. "Delicious! Guilt makes for the best nightmares. I'll suck yours out like marrow from a bone."

"That's where yer wrong." Pete shot Shadewick Gloom a look that *should* have sent him to the Realms

Below. "Ye are the one who made Lars grovel, all right, but he stood up to yer blasts until the bones of his skull smoked. Ye are the one who stood behind yer powers, afraid to face him skeleton to skeleton." He strode up to the shadowy skeleton until they thumped belly to empty belly. "Yer the one that tortured Lars Bones . . . not Billy!" Pete backed Gloom off with another bump and then turned to Billy. "Ye gotta swear off guilt right now, boy. It weren't yer fault!"

But Billy wasn't feeling the slightest guilt — something much darker filled him now. Rage. He clamped his bony fingers into fists.

"Silence, pirate!" Shadewick screamed, then fired a bolt at Pete. It was little more than a fizzle. Pete sidestepped the sparks easily, but he seemed more concerned with the look in Billy's eye.

"Ye have to let go of that, too, me boy. It's worse than guilt. Let's see if we can find some justice here. It'll do us both better than revenge."

Billy spun away from Gloom's next shot as Roger joined Pete's advance. Uncle Mordecai glanced from Pete to Roger to Billy and then to Gloom. His crotchetiness must have got the most of him, because he joined in too, shouting, "Leave the boy be, ya great rollicking git!"

Everyone looked at Mordecai as if he'd just dropped out of a nut tree.

"Looks like yer spent, Gloomy," Pete chuckled. "If I had me sword, ye'd be bone bits by now."

"Restrain them!" Shadewick Gloom commanded, and then, sliding by the obliging sentinels, he headed toward his bell jars. He paused in front of Grim's jar, his shadow robes gathering round him like a storm. "Hmmm, I've been going about this all wrong." He strode to his darkroom with the bell jar. "March the prisoners this way."

The sentinels herded Billy and company to the rear of the palace. When they arrived, Shadewick had already set Grim's head on the workbench and was heading toward a wall-sized aquarium at the back of the room. Blobby shapes slapped against the glass, spreading like hands on a windowpane. Gloom fished one out with a small net. The creature's tendrils sparked purples and reds as it tried to wriggle away.

Across the room, the sentinels took up positions on either side of a shadowport. A key hovered in its center as the black vortex swirled, humming a tortured pitch.

"I don't know what I was thinking," Gloom mumbled. "Should have done this long ago. Pop a dread onto Grim's head; he no longer controls his own thoughts. Then, *voilà*, time starts, and I'm the new master of death!" He shimmered with self-congratulations.

Time starts. . . . This might be it for Millicent! Worry jangled through Billy like a clock alarm.

Gloom grabbed the bottom of his net and flipped the dread over. It flopped out onto the workbench with a sickening *smack*. Tentacles snaking to Grim's head, the dread fitted itself over as if it were wiggling into a pair of tight trousers.

"That should do it," Shadewick gloated.

Inside the dread's gelatinous body, Grim's jaw was thrown open — locked in a scream. Billy closed his eyes, not in disgust, but in the deepest kind of concentration. Blue light flared around his bones. Dark sparks of eternal energy glittered over his lids.

"Time should be ticking by now. . . . How's this possible?" Gloom fussed. "You!" He whirled, pointing a talon sharp finger at Billy.

"Get that thing off Grim's head!" Pete shouted to Roger as he charged Gloom.

Roger and Mordecai pitched in behind, but Shadewick Gloom blasted them with two sputtering bolts, sending them skidding across the workbench. Everything including Grim's head was swept to the floor. He fired two more bursts at Pete and Billy, but missed.

"Why are you just standing there?" Shadewick Gloom screamed at the sentinels.

"Waiting for orders," the larger one rumbled.

"Well, grab them, imbeciles!"

With two massive swipes, the sentinels grabbed Billy and Pete and hauled them up by the collars. They didn't bother with Roger and Uncle Mordecai, who were passed out on the floor.

"Pin the pirate so I can attend to the boy." Shadewick stole to the tank and fished out another dread.

"It is our duty to obey," the sentinels answered mechanically.

Gloom approached Billy, his net squirming as much as his smile. "Seems you've acquired some of Grim's powers. That explains why time hasn't started and how you rebuffed me back at the cottage. Impressive, boy."

Billy didn't dare say anything. It was taking every link of his concentration to shackle time.

"I'm sure Miss Chippendale will be impressed, too. The Investigative Branch is itching to get their hands on your parents. Really aren't fond of defeats, you see. And where do you suppose Mommy and Daddy will end up, boy?"

This time Gloom almost got him. Billy screwed his eyes into deeper concentration.

"I'll have your whole snug little family in Nevermore soon, along with your deliciously guilty nightmares!" Gloom lifted the net above Billy's head, ready to overturn it.

But instead of shrinking in fear, Billy seemed transfixed, mumbling, "blindly obey." Then his smile lit up the room. He turned to the sentinels. "Excuse me, sirs, but isn't it against Dark Side rules to do a good deed?"

"The inquisitor would say that is so," the larger one rumbled.

"I was just wondering why you haven't arrested him?" Billy cocked his head toward Shadewick Gloom.

"Eh?" Gloom clacked back a step.

"He's been working with the Light Side Government. You heard him admit it. And Lightsiders are always doing right."

Pete's smile added to the room's sudden glow. "True enough, they wouldn't be on the Light Side unless they were judged good-deed doers."

The sentinels dropped their load and turned toward Shadewick Gloom.

"Don't listen to them. They have no authority here." Gloom stamped a shadowy boot.

"Yer thick with responsibility in helpin' the Investigative Branch. I'd be hornswoggled if they ain't awarded ye a medal by now," Pete said in a sugary voice, and then looked up over his shoulder. "Wouldn't want that inquisitor feller practicing his lashes on yer backs, would ye, lads? Why don't ye take him?"

The towering demons locked glances. After two

sizable nods, they grabbed Shadewick Gloom. But he wriggled in their grip like a gaffed marlin. And he would have gotten away, too, except for some sly skeleton thinking.

"Dump that thing on his head!" Billy cried, pointing to the net.

The sentinels wrestled it out of Gloom's hands, upending its contents onto his head. Gloom's arms fell limp to his sides and the dread burbled a gooey, "Num!"

Tossing Shadewick over his shoulder like a sack of soiled laundry, the large demon turned and marched out of the darkroom. The smaller sentinel followed.

When the crunch of their last footstep echoed away, Billy clattered over to the bench and burst into laughter.

Uncle Grim's head was nestled between Roger and Uncle Mordecai. Roger was coming around, but Uncle Mordecai was still knocked silly. "What's so funny?" the skeleton dandy asked, sitting up slowly.

"Your hat."

The dread had slipped off Grim's head and was trying its utmost to work its way over Roger's. His old top hat was crowned with a dread, looking very much like a glob of struggling pudding.

Roger scrambled up to his feet and sauntered over to the aquarium, where he examined his reflection in the glass. "Hmmmm, not very dashing." With a flick of his wrist he flipped the hat into the aquarium, where it sunk unceremoniously to the bottom. Pete chuckled quietly to himself from across the room, his eyes filled with twinkling affection.

Billy hunkered down next to Uncle Grim's exhausted but smiling face. "Well done, Billy. You kept time stopped just long enough for that dread to slide off my head."

"I was wondering why it got so easy all of a sudden. Thought I was getting as powerful as you."

"Unless I'm mistaken, you've more power than you can imagine, but I need you to promise you won't think about using it. I still need to straighten things out with Oversecretary Underhill."

"I'll do my best," Billy promised. He wasn't in an awful hurry to endanger his uncle or the rest of his family.

Grim shut his eyes again, and somewhere not far away his body breathed a sigh of relief. "Now you might want to smarten things up around here. You can begin by gathering me up. I think we'll be having company in a minute or two."

"How do you know that?" Billy asked.

"My body is riding on Fleggs. I can feel the rush of wind and his unmistakable gallop."

Chapter 24

Nevermore No More

BWANG! URG! THUMP!

Along with Mr. Brittleback's grunts and Millicent's shouts, these were the loudest sounds in Nevermore. The skeleton and Millicent were holding their own against the dreads.

Millicent screamed, "There's another one behind you!"

"Got it!" Mr. Brittleback leaped, swinging his shovel. The shot knocked the groundskeeper's head clean off its shoulders.

Millicent wished she could do more to help, but she had to content herself with cheering him on. So far, half of the nasty blobs had been sent to the Realms Below.

As Mr. Brittleback leaned on his shovel handle, thankful for the break, a swift wind kicked up dust as hoofs sparked up the carriage road. A magnificent midnight stallion cantered to a stop. Atop Fleggs sat Grim, body joyfully reunited with head, which now bore a wide smile.

"Bartemis!" Grim called down.

"Mill!" Billy poked out from behind his uncle's cloak.

"I suppose you'll need some saving, now." Grim's eyes crinkled cheerily.

"Thanks for the offer." Brittleback held the shovel by the end of its long handle. "But it won't be necessary." He wound up and, with one stroke, knocked all five dreads off their victims' heads.

Billy leaped off Fleggs and clacked over to Millicent. "How are we supposed to save you when you've gone and saved yourself?"

Millicent grinned. "Well, you could have, if you hadn't waited so long."

"Dad's going to be disappointed, after calling out the cavalry and all."

"The cavalry? You and Grim?" Millicent laughed.

"Not us. Them." Billy pointed to a column of distant figures.

Colonel Siegely led the way aboard his horse, Clattershanks, but he was overtaken by Ned, who cut a less dashing figure. The burly skeleton was mounted on a runaway horse. He looked as if he couldn't dismount soon enough, unlike the hundred stone-faced soldiers that trotted behind him.

"All that for me?" Millicent tried to wrap Billy in a hug, but her arms were only half there. He settled happily for a smile.

Grim dismounted and helped Mr. Brittleback lay the unconscious ghosts and skeletons he'd battled side by side.

"Hope they aren't tempted to give me a whack when they wake up." Mr. Brittleback grimaced, dropping the last ghost into place.

"Aside from their splitting headaches, I should think they'll be most thankful." Grim strode up the line to examine several ghosts laid out on the end.

"Boosborough, Sheets, Ghostly, and White. You can't say Shadewick Gloom hasn't a sense of humor: turning the most senior members of the High Council into groundskeepers."

"Cornelia Chippendale will be mighty surprised when these gentlemen return." Mr. Brittleback clattered from one groundskeeper to the next, sprucing up their clothing as best he could.

"Chippendale!" Millicent turned to Billy. "She was here. She was the one who sent Shadewick Gloom to get us in the first place, and she was really mad that he hadn't captured you, too."

"A witness tying Chippendale to the Dark Side. That's sure to help," Mr. Brittleback chirped.

"Yes." Grim tapped his chin. "But I'm not sure that's enough. Chippendale is slippery as eel sweat. I don't want any surprises when we face her. For example why was she after Billy and Millicent?"

Why? Billy tapped his own chin, unaware of how well he was copying his uncle.

"She loves her power," Mr. Brittleback mumbled. "Been clawing her way to the top of the council ever since Pickerel disappeared."

Billy met Millicent's glance.

"Chippendale knows about Pickerel!" Billy blurted.

"And she knows that *we* know," Millicent added right behind him.

"That's got to be it," Grim agreed, "but how did she find out? I know I didn't blab."

While Grim chewed on this, Pete, Mr. Bones, Roger, and Colonel Siegely arrived on skeleton horseback.

Mr. Bones smiled at Billy and Millicent. "I might have known you'd have things sorted out by the time we arrived."

"Aye, got to say they make a wily pair." Pete nudged Mr. Bones in the ribs and Jenkins smiled at the children like he'd just hatched them from two eggs.

Billy skipped over to the riders. "The missing council members!"

"Hah! Like to see Chippendale wriggle out of this one . . . blaming all this on me when she was the one who disappeared 'em." Pete dismounted with surprising grace for a bandy-legged sea dog. "We should round 'em up and parade 'em under her nose this second —"

"Not quite so fast, Pete," Mr. Bones interrupted. "We have a little more business to attend to." He nodded toward Millicent, who was drifting as fast as she could toward a nearby tomb.

"She won't leave without her parents," Billy said.

Mr. Bones swung his mount toward Clattershanks and spoke to Colonel Siegely, "Do you think your men could give us a hand?"

"My men, Mr. Bones, will be glad to give you hands, heads, and everything they've got." A few crisp commands later, the soldiers galloped off to the surrounding tombs. Backing their skeleton horses up to the doors, they bashed them in. After trotting inside, they emerged with blinking but very happy prisoners.

The first released were Millicent's parents, Artemis and Julia Hues. They met Millicent, still struggling toward the tomb, and wrapped her up in a long hug.

Millicent and her parents drifted back over to Billy, Pete, and Uncle Grim. Mr. Bones and Roger rode off with the soldiers to help release prisoners.

Soon, hundreds of stunned prisoners were milling around, with more on the way.

"Now that ye got yer parents in tow, Millicent, I'd surely like to be off to the council," Pete urged.

Grim patted Billy's and Millicent's backs. "We should have the upper hand now. Still, I'd love to know who Chippendale's ears are on Earth."

That became clear only a second later when Billy

saw a ragged red robe snaking between conversations in the crowd.

"That thing would know." He pointed to the swelling manifestation.

"I just bet Gossip would." Grim nodded. "Why else would it be here unless Chippendale was covering her tracks?" Grim waved at two ghosts standing near Gossip. "I say, gentlemen, mind lending a hand?"

Each one took an elbow and escorted the manifestation toward Grim.

"Now we just need a few golden wishes"— Grim rooted in his pockets and came up empty —"so we can get to the council."

A gold coin tumbled through the air and *tinked* off Grim's head. Billy snatched it before it hit the ground.

"Is that what you're looking for, brother?" Mr. Bones smiled down from his skeleton horse, having returned with more prisoners. "I had to borrow a few to save your bacon."

"Rifling through my things and taking what's not yours. Just like when we were kids." Grim grinned back.

Mr. Bones deposited the rest of the coins in his brother's hand, then turned to Billy, pride filling his face and his puffed-out chest. "But it was Billy who really saved you."

Billy's eyes glistened as he raked his foot through a dry clump of Nevermore leaves.

"You silly old sausage," Millicent whispered, pushing Billy, "get over there and give him a hug. Honestly," she turned to her mother, "boys!"

"And fathers." Julia Hues stroked her daughter's independent curls.

Billy walked shyly to his dad and was soon swept off his feet in his bony embrace.

Chapter 25
The Boneyard Ablaze

High Council Highlights
by Headley B. Moan

For the first time in recent memory, the High Council chambers were opened to visitors as Oversecretary Underhill challenged the extra-constitutional powers granted to Temporary Commissioner Chippendale.

To Miss Chippendale's amazement and the surprise of the rest of the council, Misters Boosborough, Sheets, Ghostly, and White — the four missing members of the council — reported for duty.

Miss Chippendale resorted to a number of procedural maneuvers to delay the proceedings, but Oversecretary Underhill and a few of his knowledgeable assistants deftly blocked each motion.

It became clear early on that Miss Chippendale's claims against Glass-Eyed Pete were false. The missing council members insisted he had nothing to do with their disappearance. And they were highly suspicious of any other charges leveled against the old pirate.

When Justice, who presides at all council sessions, asked Miss Chippendale if she had any evidence to support her case, Miss Chippendale declined to answer on the grounds that the information was top secret.

Justice asked the missing council members to testify. Their stories were most unsettling. Each told how an unknown assailant had knocked him unconscious, and about awaking in Nevermore to find he was a captive of Shadewick Gloom.

Miss Chippendale interrupted the testimony repeatedly to accuse Mr. Gloom of crimes against deceased humanity. She said she was convinced that it was Shadewick Gloom who was behind all of this wickedness and that she needed even more power to confront this Dark Side menace.

Oversecretary Underhill suggested that Miss Chippendale was blaming someone who was conveniently not there and unable to defend himself. He also reminded the council that this had not been the first time she had used that ploy.

The most unusual highlight of the day came when Master Billy Bones Biglum and Miss Millicent Hues, two youngsters from Earth, took the stand.

The children testified about Shadewick Gloom's visit to Earth to steal Miss Hues's soul. While this was a black mark against Shadewick Gloom, it didn't do much to discredit Miss Chippendale. It wasn't until Miss Hues testified that she had seen Miss Chippendale in Nevermore that things got interesting.

Miss Chippendale tried to wish herself away, but was restrained by Grim Bones, the Hall of Reception's chief field agent and the presiding angel of death.

Justice declared that Temporary Commissioner Chippendale should be taken into custody by Oversecretary Underhill until there could be a thorough housecleaning at the Investigative Branch.

The session was adjourned and it is this reporter's opinion that for the first time, in a very long while, Justice smiled.

"Nearly popped my vest buttons when I read this, Billy. Your mother's going to be proud, too." Mr. Bones folded the paper with an expert crease and placed it on

the table. "And we're quite proud of you, too, my dear."
He smiled at Millicent.

The three of them were sitting at a table in the
Boneyard. The table was barely recognizable with its
high sheen and elaborate spread of Afterlife delicacies.
But the table didn't hold a candle to the rest of the
place.

Mrs. Lumbus had not been shy with her golden
wishes, now that Pete had paid back all he owed. The
old tavern glittered with fantastic strands of colorful
flowers ablaze in twinkling lights. The place was packed.
Not only with the heroes of the day like Grim, Pete,
Roger, and Ned, but also many neighbors who had been
drawn by the smells and the wonderful music.

Millicent's mother and father hadn't been up to the festivities after their ordeal in Nevermore. They were spending a quiet evening at their charming little home in Nightbridge, one of the poshest neighborhoods in Celesdon. Millicent and Billy had promised to stop by for a private celebration with them before heading back to Earth.

Billy could barely hear himself think with the gales of laughter and the tinkling glasses of ale being skillfully spilled down the skeleton's gullets and recaptured in glasses held in their ribcages below.

Liam Slackbones and Ned were hitting it off spectacularly well at a table at the back of the room. They sang lusty songs while pounding out the beat on the table. An unexpected guest was there, too. Uncle Mordecai. He had spent a good deal of the evening trotting after Grim, thanking him over and over for giving him a second chance at judgment procedures.

For most of the party, Grim had been trying to make his way to Billy's table, but every time he closed in, someone would sweep him away into a conversation. It was not too surprising, as everyone wanted to rub shoulders with one of the most powerful beings in the Afterlife. Grim was pleasant enough, but growing weary of all the hobnobbing.

And Roger Jolly had also been delayed as girl after skeleton girl grabbed his bony hands and pulled him onto the dance floor. He was so exhausted after twenty-something dances that he stumbled back to his table and promptly sat on his brand-new top hat.

Mrs. Lumbus was wearing a red velvet dress adorned in bows. She and Pete were seated at bar. She had his arm locked between her own as they chatted quietly, gazing into each other's eyes. Jenkins seemed a bit bored by the whole thing and found perch on the rim of a bowl of pirate grog. Every so often, he rolled his eyes at the lovebirds.

Billy heard a hearty "Haw, haw, haw." He turned to see Colonel Siegely. With his boot up on a chair, he could have been posing for a sculptor. The colonel was regaling a rather comely skeleton girl with his tales of heroics. But he kept glancing around the room like he was hoping to see someone else.

"Now what are you smiling at?" Millicent wanted to know.

Billy was a little embarrassed to say, but she finally got it out of him.

"I saw Gramps Pete in a dress." The confounded look on her face prompted him to tell her how they had made it through the Gate of Darkness, and how it seemed that Colonel Siegely had developed an other-worldly crush.

A bout of the giggles kept them occupied for a good long time.

Just as the party was winding down, a detachment of skeleton guards marched through the front door. Their uniforms were similar to Grim's: polished boots, black tunics, and visored caps punctuated with silver winged skulls.

Oversecretary Underhill swept in next, in his billowing robes. The guards took up discrete posts around the room while Underhill paid his respects to his hostess. "I am so sorry to be late, my dear Mrs. Lumbus, but as you can imagine with the added responsibilities, things are rather busy at the department right now."

"You're welcome at any hour, Oversecretary." She curtsied.

Mr. Bones jumped up, herding Billy and Millicent over to the bar. Oversecretary Underhill made a sweeping bow as they approached.

"Lars Bones, my good man. Thank you so much for consenting to stay for the celebrations. We couldn't have the guests of honor leaving quite so soon."

The tall skeleton with the high forehead nodded

regally at Billy and Millicent. Millicent curtsied at once, and Billy bobbed a bow after a gentle nudge from Mr. Bones.

"We owe you a great debt of thanks, children."

"You're welcome, Mr. Underhill," Billy said. "And thanks again for getting my mom and dad out of Nevermore last year."

"Sorry about that, sir." Mr. Bones jumped in. "We've been remiss in teaching him all the Afterlife ways." He whispered to Billy, "Call him Oversecretary Underhill, or your lordship, Billy, *not* Mr. Underhill."

"Lars! Please don't embarrass the boy. It's quite all right," Oversecretary Underhill scolded gently. "We won't stand on ceremony. But we will stand for a toast!" Underhill grabbed a glass from a floating tray and raised it high. "Ladies and gentlemen. I give you Billy and Millicent. Heroes of the day!"

A great "Huzzah!" went up around the room, as did the bottom of every glass.

By the tail end of the party, Grim had managed to make it to Billy's and Millicent's table. He sat facing them now. Mr. Bones was by the bar conferring with

Underhill as he prepared to join the stream of departing guests.

"What's to become of Miss Chippendale?" It was a question that had been on Billy's mind since she had been marched from the High Council chambers.

"Interesting that you ask." Grim threw an arm across the back of his chair and looked across the room. "It's what Oversecretary Underhill and your dad are discussing. The Oversecretary thinks the High Council made a mistake when they shipped Shadewick Gloom to the Dark Side. And he's sure Chippendale is too tricky to keep in the Hall of Reception or the Department of Fibs and Fabrications."

"What will they do with her?" Millicent asked.

"He's charging Billy's mom and dad with an extra duty. They're to look after her. Much of this started with the disappearance of Commissioner Pickerel, and that's where it will end."

Billy and Millicent shared a look.

"You're going to jam her into the magical vase with Pickerel?" Billy asked, the corners of his bony mouth curling up.

"No, nephew." Grim patted Billy's hand. "*You* are, when we return to Earth. You did such a good job before, Underhill won't trust it to anyone else."

"That vase is going to get a little crowded." Millicent chuckled.

"More than a little, I suspect. We'll march her to the manor, and that's where she'll stay, bottled up — far away from any possible Afterlife allies.

"Billy, Chippendale and Pickerel couldn't be under better care. Your parents are the most trusted secrets-closet skeletons in the D.F.F. Bet you can't wait to get back."

"I wish we could show Millicent all of Celesdon before we go." Billy sighed. "It's so beautiful."

"You'll show her as much of it as you want, Billy." Grim stood up, slipping on his leather gloves. "During my next vacation, I should think. I'm sanctioned to stop time at least once a year for my week-long break. The two of you can visit then."

"Really?" Millicent's curls jigged.

"Really," Grim assured her.

"How's that for an adventure?" Billy grinned.

Grim bid them farewell in a huge hug, grabbed his Cloak of Doom from the rack, and disappeared in the midst of flinging it around his shoulders. When Billy and Millicent heard Fleggs's distant whinny, they knew he was really gone.

The talk of awaiting adventure reminded Billy of why they had wanted to contact Pete in the first place. Billy and Millicent pulled him away from Mrs. Lumbus just long enough to plead their case.

"Ye want a few weeks on the *Spurious II*, do ye?" Pete rubbed his stubbly chin. "I wouldn't mind bangin' over waves for a spell meself." He shot a smile at Mrs. Lumbus. "But I'll miss this little flower too much if I stay longer."

Billy and Millicent did their best to not burst into laughter seeing the old pirate smitten so.

"I'll be glad to plead yer case with Mum Biglum. Who knows, maybe she'll want to come along? She ain't shy when it comes to adventures. Leastwise not when she was a young 'un."

"Really?" Billy blinked.

"Now where do ye think ye two get yer love for far-flung adventures? Outta thin air?" Pete chuckled.

"We were thinking it came from you," Millicent said.

"I'd love to think it was all from me, but the old girl's packed with a hold full of surprises. I'll just have to remind her."

And so, just a month later, the residents of Barmouth stepped out of their front doors and peered out of shop-windows. They had gathered to watch a tall ship cast off from its berth and tip elegantly into the wind.

A boy and girl raced to the ship's bow and then leaned over the rail as if they could beat the ship to its first port of call. An old woman hobbled up behind them, her cane raised like a sword pointing to the horizon.

And there were some in town, who swore for years to come, they saw a pirate floating just above the children. With chest thrust out and arms tucked behind, it looked as if he owned every drop in the sea.